Facing the Lutha

MJ Haag

Facing the Lutha
Copyright: MJ Haag
Published: April 4, 2017
ISBN: 978-1-544057-91-0
Cover Design: Shattered Glass Publishing

Titles by Melissa Haag

Zepher's gone missing, and Tink needs to determine why before she has another situation on her hands. The voices in her head are warning her to look deeper at her community, and what she learns isn't good. She and Rogan haven't yet escaped the influence of the girdack, and Zepher's disappearance is just the beginning of the trouble waiting for them. Only one thing can possibly save her family: facing the Lutha.

One

I moved to Rogan's side and watched the males leave.

"What do you think the Lutha will do when they return without you?" I asked.

Rogan chuckled and wrapped his arms around me. It felt so good to be touched that I sighed and leaned close, inhaling his scent.

"She'll scramble to pick some other unlucky soul to mate her crazy daughter."

"You don't mind giving up the community, the power?"

"Hell no. I'm relieved they're finally going back with the message I've been telling them all along. There was no way in hell I was ever going to accept the Lutha's daughter."

Relief filled me. Although he'd said the words before, I knew how our kind worked. Power and control. Shows of dominance. I'd thought I'd been alone in my dislike of it all.

"Good," I said. "Now, let's go home. You smell like bacon, and I'm hungry."

He laughed, kissed the top of my head, and kept an arm

around my shoulders as we slowly walked the streets.

Hunger woke me.

Warm and comfortably laying on my side, I opened my eyes. Rogan's peaceful, sleep-relaxed face greeted me. A dark sweep of hair covered his forehead, and a small smile tugged his mouth. An intense stirring rushed through me, and I licked my lips where the taste of him still lingered. Mine, mated and won. How had I gotten so lucky?

He was everything I'd wanted but had never hoped for. Our short time together felt more like a dream, and I struggled to suppress the urge to wake him and take him again just to prove he was real and mine. Since our first mating, this possessive feeling gripped me often, reminding me of what I was trying not to be. A crazy bitch in heat, fighting the descent.

Easing from the bed, I reached for my discarded pajamas. The modest, button-up top with the matching pants hadn't stayed on long. Rogan liked undressing me as much as I liked to throw him on the bed. The images of both scenes had my skin tingling with the need, and the urge to wake him up and start again rode me harder.

Although the voice was gone, the lessons remained. Control, I reminded myself quietly. Rogan rolled over in his sleep, dislodging the sheet covering his waist. I stared again, tempted, then forced myself to leave the bedroom. I needed to push my obsession with Rogan aside for a few hours. My community depended on me. I had responsibilities.

My stomach growled as I opened the refrigerator and pulled a dozen eggs off the otherwise empty shelves. Another reminder I was obsessed with Rogan.

I had the scrambled eggs cooking in the pan when I heard Rogan in the bedroom. My focus shifted from the food to listening for him. The whisper of sound in the hall had me tensing in anticipation.

"Control," I said softly.

"Why did you leave?" he asked, walking into the kitchen.

A shiver chased over my skin at the huskiness of his voice. I didn't acknowledge my reaction, but he did. He grabbed me from behind, and I closed my eyes at the feel of his chest pressed against my back. His scent wrapped around me and made my mouth water.

No. Stay focused.

"I think we've spent enough time in bed," I said, steadily.

"Hardly." His lips brushed the side of my neck as his hand glided over my side and around to the front of my shirt, deftly sliding under it so his fingers stroked the skin around my navel.

"We need to eat." Despite my words, I shut off the burner and put a cover on the cooking eggs.

No matter how much I knew I should deny him, I was too hungry for him again. Our mating, only a day old, still held me in its thrall. I craved his obedience and his body. He'd given me both, many times over, and it hadn't even started to satiate the need. Not that I'd admit it to him or anyone else.

I liked Rogan as a person and as a mate. I respected the hard choice he'd made leaving the girdack. But what I felt for him at the moment had nothing to do with any of that. The need clawing at my insides was primal. Aggressive.

Consuming. And it rubbed the lifestyle I'd chosen the wrong way. I wanted to be so much better than what I was. For my community and for Rogan.

"I knew I'd win," he said with a chuckle when I turned in his arms and kissed him hard.

The sound of Kye's feet hitting the stairs had Rogan groaning against my lips. I pulled back with a forced grin.

"What was that about winning?"

The little girl stepped through the door and made a small sound of annoyance, like a mini Shay.

"Is that all you do now?" Kye asked. "Shay said she's leaving in ten minutes if you want a ride."

Her words cooled the need that continued to tear at my insides.

The result of my choice of methods when dealing with Bull had landed Will and Denz in the hospital; and, today, they could come home. Shay planned to pick them up, and I'd offered to go with her. There were medical bills to pay and amends to make. I wasn't looking forward to visiting the hospital and facing the consequence of my actions but knew it needed to be done.

Rogan watched me closely, waiting for my decision.

"Will you grab the plates?" I asked him. He reluctantly released me, and I looked at Kye. "Let your aunt know we'll be right down."

"All right." She didn't move to leave.

I studied her for a moment, noting the sadness reflecting in her brown eyes, and opened myself to her thoughts and feelings. With one brother in the hospital because of Bull and me spending all my time with Rogan, Kye was lonely. Guilt tightened my chest. I was shirking my responsibilities to my community.

"Would you like to help me bake a pie when I get back?" I asked while Rogan plated our breakfast.

Kye nodded, and her immediate happiness touched my mind. Over something so simple. Kindness and my time.

"Then, I'll leave some money with Rogan, and the two of you can shop while I'm gone."

"What kind of pie?" Rogan asked, not questioning my sudden decision to leave him behind. He was perfect.

He blatantly licked my fork before handing me a plate of food. Perfect and naughty.

"We're out of apples," he said with an even naughtier grin. He'd fed them to me as snacks between matings.

I looked down at my plate and fought to subdue my reignited hunger for him.

"I'll let you two decide," I said, my voice surprisingly even.

My hunger didn't fade so easily when each bite of breakfast tasted like him. Yet, as I quickly ate and listened to him and Kye debate between apple and pumpkin, I couldn't mind. Our connection grounded me, just as my community did. I needed both to stay sane.

As soon as I finished, I took my plate to the sink before retreating to the bedroom and closing the door. The sheets where a rumpled tangle. Years of keeping things neat demanded I remake the bed. However, the scent of our sweat and sex drove me crazy. I picked up his pillow and breathed in.

From the kitchen, I heard Rogan and Kye's change in conversation.

"Why she sending me with you? Still need a babysitter?" the little girl asked.

I set the pillow down and pulled the sheet straight as I listed for his reply.

"Yep. Tink likes me and knows you'll keep me from running away."

"You thinking about running?"

I paused straightening the blankets.

"Every time Tink looks my direction," he said.

Aggression surfaced at his words. I wanted to bare my teeth and lock him in the bedroom with me to prove his statement untrue.

Control is power.

I shook my head to dislodge the thought and moved away from the bed. I didn't need to control him or prove his words false. He was teasing because he knew I could hear. He'd learn not to do that.

Focusing on my closet, I considered the meager selection of clothes before me and pulled out the most respectable skirt and blouse. The bitter tang of bleach and other chemicals still clung to the material as I dressed. It was a relief that I no longer needed to hide my scent. That I would never need to use bleach again. Rogan had freed me.

Dressed in a pencil skirt and button-up, collared blouse, I reemerged from the bedroom. Rogan's gaze hungrily followed me, and the growing bulge in the front of his jeans made my mouth water. He knew what the scent of his arousal would do to me and needed to control himself. I'd remind him of that when I returned.

"Behave, Rogan," I said as I passed him.

"I am," he said innocently, giving Kye a wink as the girl looked between us with curiosity.

I picked up my purse and fished through the neatly bundled rolls of bills I'd collected before Rogan's appearance. There was plenty in there. I took one bundle and tossed it to Rogan.

"Kye, make sure he shops smart."

"I'm right here," he said, frowning at the bundle of bills.

"I know you are. But I also know you probably haven't had to shop for groceries on your own. Kye has experience with saving money."

He held up the bundle. "And, we need to save?"

"We do. Money isn't easy to earn here. It needs to last a very long time."

The loss of a large portion of money when I settled the hospital bill would hurt the community. Just another consequence of my actions, I thought as I put on my jacket.

It wasn't just my money I carried in the purse but theirs as well. Money that provided heat, shelter and food for those having a hard time providing for themselves. And, although I knew that Will and Denz were covered by some kind of health insurance, I wouldn't allow Shay or Denz's mom to carry the burden of what remained.

"Take care of each other," I said as I moved to step out the door. A tug on my jacket stopped me.

I glanced down and saw Rogan's hand. He turned me and

gave me a hard kiss.

"You're not alone anymore," he said softly against my lips. "We will care for our community together. And, Kye will teach me to shop."

Was I so easy for him to read now?

"Damn straight," the little girl said.

I kissed Rogan, savoring the taste of him, then stepped away.

"Kye, no swearing," I said.

She nodded, and I went down to Shay, who was waiting by the door. A knowing grin tugged at Shay's mouth.

"You sure you want to come with me? You and that man of yours seem like you could use more alone time."

I didn't want to go with her; I needed to.

"There will be time later," I said.

Shay remained quiet as we got into her car and she started toward the hospital. When she stopped at an intersection, the space between my shoulders blades tingled with unease. I looked around, but the streets were empty, which was normal given the early hour.

The tingle continued to tickle the skin covering my spine, and I opened myself, trying to determine the source. Shay's worry and fears poured into me. She was struggling to keep all three of her sister's children happy and healthy and was wondering what life she would have left when she was done. Seeing me with Rogan had reminded her of what she was missing. Yet, her sense of responsibility to those kids wouldn't allow her to do anything but give all of herself to their care.

When the car moved forward, I closed myself from her

thoughts and feelings; and the unease slowly started to fade. By the time she parked in the large lot, I felt more relaxed.

Human hospitals were an odd place. The chemical smells mixed with the unhappy thoughts and feelings probably should have depressed me. Instead, it all reminded me that nothing in life was meant to be easy. Whether I wanted to or not, I needed to fight to survive. Fight to be happy.

As soon as we walked through the doors, I went to settle the bill, and Shay went to collect the boys. The woman at the payment desk said nothing as I counted out almost two thousand dollars in twenties. She handed me a receipt, which I tucked into my much lighter purse. I'd need to do another job much sooner than I would have liked. If only I would have seen this potential outcome when I'd confronted Bull that first time.

A squeak to my right drew my attention, and I turned to see the elevator open. My anger spiked at seeing Will and Denz wheeled out. Neither looked significantly damaged from where I stood, but I knew better. I'd seen them bleeding and lying in the alley. My people. My friends. Hurt because of my skewed judgment. It wouldn't happen again. My head was finally clear, and I'd protect my community better, now.

"Hey, tiny Tink," Will said with a grin. "What do you think of my wheels?"

"I don't care for them or the hospital. I'm sorry for what you've suffered."

"Suffered? Nah, I got this hot nurse to give me a backrub and her number last night."

The image of the nurse filled my mind. A small brunette

with pale skin and a big bust.

"She's older than you by seven years and has a small child. Are you prepared for that?" I asked.

Some of the humor left Will's face. Although I didn't regret my pragmatic words, I regretted his lost humor. He'd only spoken to try to alleviate my guilt.

"I'll go get the car," Shay said with a pat to Denz's shoulder.

Left alone with the two boys and the nurses pushing their chairs, I quietly waited for Shay's car to appear outside the doors.

A feeling of unease tickled the skin between my shoulder blades again as I stared out the windows. I opened myself, but Will and Denz were content. I opened myself wider, listening to those around me. Nothing in their thoughts justified the growing apprehension I felt.

ROGAN

Kye pushed the cart through the store, as usual, and gave me another lesson in shopping. We didn't spend all the money, but I bought more food than any of the previous trips. And a lot of apples.

Ambrey's appetites were large and hard to satisfy. I was up for the task, though. Anytime. Anywhere. I grinned thinking about the last time I satisfied her.

"You're not listening again," Kye said, slapping my arm. "And why you grinnin' like that?"

"Sorry. Thinking about Tink."

The little girl rolled her eyes.

"I asked how we're going to get all this back to apartment."

"Think Georgy will let us take the cart?"

"No. Tink doesn't allow it because the store loses too many carts that way."

"Guess we'll just need to man up and carry it all, then."

She rolled her eyes at me again, and I chuckled.

"You two officially hooked up now?" she asked, heading toward the checkout.

"Yep. You okay with that?"

"I guess. She's never hooked up before. It's weird seeing her so..." The little girl frowned.

"Happy?" I said.

"Distracted." Kye gave me an annoyed look then started unloading the groceries. I loved shopping with her.

"Adults sometimes get distracted. It never lasts forever."

"You already planning on dumping her?" The outrage in Kye's voice made me laugh.

"No. Tink and I are together for life."

"Whoa. Slow down. A few days together isn't long enough to start talking about getting married. Even I know that."

Amused, but smart enough to keep it to myself, I finished unloading the cart and paid. More than half of the rolled up bills went back into my pocket. The money made me curious. Since coming here, I hadn't seen Ambrey work. Sure, she did a lot for her community, but she had no human job that I'd noticed. I couldn't help but wonder how she'd gotten so much money. I was tempted to ask Kye but figured I'd annoyed her enough for a while.

Georgy double bagged everything, and I looped bags around my arms until I was out of arm room and carrying half my weight in food. Kye looked at the remaining bags and shook her head.

"I'm strong, but not that strong."

"We'll do two trips then. It'll be fun."

"Your idea of fun is messed up," she said, grabbing three bags.

Georgy set the rest aside for us, and we stepped out of the store into the rising wind. Grey clouds swirled above us.

"I am not walking back in the rain," Kye grumbled. I chuckled and walked beside her as she set out at a brisk pace.

By the time we reached the apartment, Shay's car was parked out front. Kye saw it, and her dragging steps had a sudden new burst of energy to them.

"Just leave the bags on the stairs, Kye," I said when she opened the door. "I'll come back and get them."

She quickly dropped the bags and ran down the hall to her apartment. Her excited voice carried to me as I started up the steps with my load.

I couldn't blame her for her excitement. She hadn't seen her brother for almost three days because of the accident, while I'd only been apart from Ambrey for a few hours and struggled to contain the need crawling through me. I took the steps two at a time.

The door at the top stood open, and I saw Ambrey in the

living room. She had her back to the apartment door and was staring out the living room window. As I watched, she twisted her arm behind her back, in a very nimble move, and scratched at the spot between her shoulder blades. Something about the way she did it hinted at agitation. Had she missed me like I'd missed her?

Although the sharp tang of old bleach still clouded the air, it wasn't enough to mask her scent anymore. I inhaled, searching for her fragrance like a starved man, while I hurried to put away groceries.

When I finished, I was so focused on reaching her that I didn't at first notice the stiff tension in her shoulders.

"Ambrey?"

She turned from the window, her troubled gaze meeting mine.

"Something's wrong. I can feel it but don't know what it is."

I wrapped her in my arms, needing to touch and offer comfort as much as receive it. With everything we'd faced, she'd never looked troubled like this.

The tension left her shoulders as she hugged me in return.

"Talk to me. Tell me what happened," I said, smoothing my hand over her silky hair.

"Nothing. We went to the hospital, picked up the boys, and came back here."

Yet, there was a hint of concern laced in her words.

"Why do you think something's wrong?"

She pulled back and looked at me.

"Do you know how I won their trust and respect?" she asked.

I shook my head.

"With a touch, I can see into a person. Know what they are thinking and feeling."

Females all had strength and sharpened senses because of their connection to the moon. However, I'd never heard of any admitting to psychic abilities. Our kind was known for shifting and solidarity, nothing else. Yet, I wasn't foolish enough to doubt her.

"Even me?" I asked. Then, I started picturing our time together in the shower.

"Yes. And you're not helping right now," she said with a prim look that only drove my need for her higher.

I imagined bending her over the bed. Me dominating her. Her pupils immediately dilated.

"You need to control yourself." An edge of command laced her words.

"What we have is too new, Ambrey. I'm trying, but there's a reason newly mated pairs aren't seen for almost a week." I wasn't making excuses. This need to be with her, to please her in any way possible, was exactly why I'd run from the Lutha and her plans for me. To feel this with anyone but Ambrey would have been hell.

I took in her neatly buttoned shirt, precise bun, and cool look with a groan.

"I can't help wanting you." I leaned in and nuzzled her neck. "Maybe that's what you're feeling. Our separation."

She growled, turned me, and pushed me down onto the

couch.

"Don't move," she said.

When she strode to the door and locked it, I stayed on the couch, an eager grin spreading across my face.

Two

TINK

Panting, I fell face first into the mattress and Rogan collapsed on top of me. He pressed his lips to my shoulder then neck.

If the uneasiness still prickled between my shoulders, I couldn't tell as he slowly moved within me.

"We can't stay in here all morning." My words were muffled. I turned my head to repeat them.

"We can, and you want to."

Again, the husky tone made me shiver. I was needy and greedy and shameless about it. Arching my hips back into his teasing thrusts, I let him distract me.

This time he was slower; and, still sensitive from the previous time, each touch, lick, and nip drove me wild. Especially the gentle ones and the way he looked into my eyes just before he kissed me.

Most women cared about how strong a man was. Not me. I cared about how gentle he could be. How understanding and thoughtful. So far, Rogan seemed to have it all. And he was mine. I basked in his attention and returned it as gently as I could. It wasn't always easy. The need to dominate him still tried to put my wishes in the back seat. But I maintained control. For him. I'd seen matings where the male emerged bruised or broken, and I didn't want that for Rogan.

However, when someone knocked on the door, my restraint slipped, and rage clawed its way to the surface as Rogan started to withdraw. I snarled and flipped him onto the bed. In the next second, I was straddling him.

"No." A growl accompanied the word.

"Ambrey, I wasn't leaving."

To prove his words, he grabbed my hips and thrust back into me. The delicious friction of each uncompromising slide and the forceful way his fingers gripped me had me growling with pleasure. My nails raked his chest as I closed my eyes and arched into the ride. The sound of our heavy breathing filled the room.

When the knock came again, his pace increased. I fell forward, planted my hands on his chest, and took everything he gave. Sweat slicked his skin and his scent bathed me. The feel of him, within and against me, pushed me over. I cried out as I crested and bonelessly fell to the side when he moved under me.

It took several breaths to realize Rogan was no longer in the room. Annoyance flared. Outside, thunder rumbled and rain lashed the windows, matching my mood.

"Rogan?"

"Just a second," he called.

I heard the rustle of plastic, then the door closed and the locked turned. Standing, I walked naked to the kitchen.

Rogan had his jeans on and was putting away groceries.

"I thought you already put those away."

He looked back at me, his expression going from serious to puppy in a second. I didn't try to cover the places his gaze lingered. I waited until he'd swallowed hard, looked his fill, then met my gaze.

"We had too many for one trip and left some at the store. I got distracted and forgot about the rest on the steps, too," he said, his voice rough.

"Who brought what you forgot and left behind?"

"Kye and Calem."

He put away the last item without breaking his gaze from mine then stalked across the room. It didn't matter that I had been thoroughly satisfied only minutes ago. I watched him hungrily, regardless. The way he moved, each easy step called attention to the jeans riding low on his hips. I licked my lips and let my gaze rove the delicious expanse of his hairy chest.

When he reached me, I gently touched the angry red furrows that ran just inside of each nipple. Evidence of lost control. Why, then, did the sight of them excited me more?

"I'm sorry about these."

"Really? I was hoping for another set."

I met his amused gaze and shook my head.

"I still feel out of control," I admitted.

"I know. It's part of who you are."

I sighed heavily. "I know. And I hate it."

ROGAN

Her hazel gaze begged for understanding. There was nothing for me to understand. Only her.

"Don't hate who you are. Because you're perfect. In every way."

I smoothed my hands down her arms and stepped close, ready to prove how much I loved her losing control with me. Movement outside the window distracted me before I could kiss her.

In the storm-darkened streets, a figure stood alone. When I lifted my head, the figure lifted one arm, holding out something round. The wind shifted just then, changing the direction of the rain so the object swung and turned slightly at the same time lightning flashed.

"Shit."

I stepped past Ambrey and pressed closer to the window to see clearer, but between one blink and the next, whatever I'd seen was gone.

"What was that?" Ambrey asked, standing behind me but leaning around, trying to see.

Bile churned in my stomach and tried to creep up my throat as the details of the image remained firmly imbedded in my mind's eye.

"We need to get dressed." I turned and strode to the bedroom.

Socks and shirt were on the floor. I tugged them on as Ambrey did the same with her clothes.

"Tell me what you saw," she said.

19

"I don't know what I saw." And I was too afraid to voice my suspicions.

She followed me to the door and grabbed my arm when I reached for my shoes.

"Tell me what you think you saw," she repeated.

I met her gaze.

"A person holding a head." Hearing it aloud made me sound crazy. Who would actually walk around with someone's head?

Ambrey's expression turned angry.

"Not this time." She turned away, took her jacket from the hook, and hurried to put it on.

"This time? This has happened before?" I yanked my shoes on as she grabbed an umbrella and slipped on her flats.

"No one has been beheaded that I'm aware of. I meant I don't want anyone else hurt."

I finished tying my shoes just as she opened the door and marched down the stairs. I hustled to catch up.

Rain lashed at my face as soon as we opened the entrance. Ambrey didn't bother with the umbrella but strode determinedly down the sidewalk.

"Tell me where," she said.

We walked a fair distance down the road before I stopped and looked back at the building.

"About here."

Ambrey turned a slow circle, looking at everything. The blacktop. The sidewalk. The buildings.

"Too much water," she said. "There's no trace of anything. Not even the normal stink of this place."

"What do we do?"

"Make sure everyone's safe."

Ambrey strode to the nearest building and let herself in. The long hallway went straight toward a set of stairs leading up. At the top was a single door. She knocked briskly as water dripped from us onto the dark, thin carpet.

The door swung open after a minute to reveal a balding man with a belly so large, skin peaked from under his shirt. The expression on his face changed from annoyance to nothing at the sight of Ambrey.

"Tink," he said in a deep voice.

"Rogan thinks he spotted a stranger. A dangerous one. Start the calls. I'll walk the community. No one goes out alone. Groups of five or more only. Use the air horns."

He nodded, a frown of concern appearing on his face as he looked from Ambrey to me then back.

"Do you want mine?" he asked.

"We'll be fine. Tell the rest."

She turned, and I moved aside to let her back down the stairs.

"Stay out of her way," the big man said softly when I moved to follow her.

I nodded once and left. She waited for me in the rain.

"Air horns?" I said.

"After I won them over, I prepared them as best as I could."

"For what?"

"For our kind. For me."

She started walking, and I fell into step beside her. Rain

whipped into our faces with stinging aggression. It didn't seem to faze her.

"My mother drilled into me the dangers of the descent. When I settled here and started to care for these people, I knew I had to do something in case I lost myself completely or any of our kind found me."

"What good is an air horn?"

"You saw what happened when Kye whistled. The air horn will do the same. Together, they will stand more of a chance than apart. Even crazy, we know the dangers of exposing our race."

"Do you think that's what I saw? One of our own?"

"I don't know. You thought you saw someone holding a head. Human or werewolf, that isn't good."

She was right, but one was definitely much worse for us than the other.

We walked to the next building. The first door Ambrey knocked on hadn't yet received a call, so she told the woman the same thing, walked to the next apartment in the building, and repeated the message to start making calls.

"Do they all have each other's phone numbers?" I asked.

"Yes. There's a list by block and building. They'll pick a block further from here and start calling. This was the fastest way I could think of to alert the community of danger. Each call will grow the network of those aware of the danger and increase the number of people spreading the news. We'll walk the community, knocking on the first door of each building until we start hearing a different answer."

After the last apartment in the building was aware, we

stepped back out into the rain. It wasn't until the fourth building that the answer changed. The man had the door open before she knocked.

"Tink, the building is aware and the residents all safely accounted for."

"Thank you."

She turned and started toward the exit without knocking on any other apartments.

"How many buildings are there?" I asked.

"Over five hundred. But we're done walking. The network has grown to the point everyone will know in about five minutes. Let's head back and wait for the call."

"What call?" I asked.

"The one that tells us who's missing."

TINK

My stomach churned as we walked back to the apartment. I was soaked through and chilled to the marrow, but it barely registered. My mind remained focused on the possibilities of what was happening in my community.

When Rogan and I had stopped in the street, there hadn't been a sign of anything. No blood or gore. No scents. I wasn't a stranger to violence. There should have been something, despite the rain. Yet, there was nothing. It would have been simpler to think Rogan had imagined what he'd seen, but he'd been touching me when he saw it. The image of the shadowy shape holding out the severed head was in my mind, too.

Someone had been out in the rain. There was the possibility of it being a prank, but that was slim. The people in my community knew better than to fake violence. We ran quarterly drills and had a system to prevent and report vicious behavior. My community understood I took the peace and well-being of our neighborhoods seriously. Our drills were perfectly timed, and if there was someone missing, Shay would have the news for me by the time I reached the door.

And it was that potential news that had my stomach twisting and the physical itch between my shoulder blades burning fiercely. Bull and many others before him had proven that humans were capable of violence, but the severity of beheading rang of our kind.

By taking Rogan from the Lutha's chosen successor, I'd started something. Rogan believed the Lutha would leave us alone and choose another mate for her daughter, Arya, but I knew better. The Lutha wouldn't take the theft so lightly. I'd gone against her wishes and there would be repercussions, but to what degree?

When I opened the door, Shay was waiting at the bottom of the stairs. Her face was free of tears, and her scent clear of sadness.

"The community is safe and the residents accounted for," she said.

"Everyone?" I asked.

She nodded, and I frowned. It didn't make sense. Could it really have been a prank?

"Was this a test?"

"No. We remain alert. No one travels alone. Groups of five or more. And, if anyone stood in the street, holding anything that might be mistaken for a severed head, they should come forward."

Shay's eyes widened, and she paled slightly. But I couldn't hold the potential truth from her. From any of them.

"Please spread the word," I said before leaving.

Rogan followed me upstairs. The apartment still smelled like sex, a distraction I didn't need.

"Can you to make lunch?" I asked as I removed my coat.

"Sure. Do you have something in mind?"

"Something big. We'll have people stopping in all day." I met his gaze. "The door will need to stay open."

Rogan nodded and leaned forward to press a chaste kiss to my forehead. I was relieved he understood and was behaving. My restraint, when it came to him, was too unstable.

"We'll be fine. Go shower and warm up. I'll handle things until you're done."

He nudged me toward the hallway, and I willingly escaped to think. The tingle of unease wasn't letting up. It was growing stronger. Something was wrong with what was happening, but what?

I let the shower warm my back and closed my eyes to focus on the frozen image still in my mind. The head mid-sway in the wind, dark and hard to see. I stopped focusing on it and looked at the person shrouded in the rain. Standing near the center of the street, very little light reached any part of the figure.

I let the whole moment, as brief as it had been, replay in my mind. The lashing, blowing rain. The slow lift of the arm. The swaying movement on the head.

The instant the lightning struck, a white-blue glow illuminated everything.

My mind caught on Zepher's decapitated head.

A pained gasp escaped me, and I slammed my hand on the faucet, shutting the water off. I stood there, dripping and in shock. Zepher. Poor Zepher. He'd lost everything because of me. Even his head. My eyes watered as I struggled to understand why someone would kill him.

I forced myself to focus on that moment again.

Blood on the lips curled in a taunting grin.

Long dark hair swept over a shoulder.

The bite mark on his cheek.

Rage lanced through me. The Lutha had decided her punishment for taking Rogan from Arya. She'd set her crazy daughter loose on my community.

I grabbed my towel. I needed to know my mind wasn't playing tricks on me.

Three

ROGAN

The bathroom door opened and slammed against the wall. I looked over my shoulder in time to see Ambrey, wrapped in nothing but a towel, dash toward the door.

"Ambrey?"

She didn't stop. I quickly turned off the burner and raced after her. She didn't go outside as I half-expected, but burst into Shay's apartment. Denz and Will occupied the sofa, and Calem and Kye sat at the table. Sandwiches still in their hands, they looked up at Ambrey's intrusion.

"You okay, Tink?" Kye asked.

Ambrey looked anything but okay. Her cheeks were pale and her eyes slightly wide.

"Where's Shay?" Ambrey said, not answering.

She took a step forward, likely to look for the woman, when a door opened down the hall.

"I'm here," the older woman said. "What is it?"

"Zepher's dead. How did we miss that?" Ambrey asked.

My stomach dropped as I realized what she was saying. The boy she'd saved from Bull was dead. I couldn't believe it. Neither could Shay. Her mouth opened for a stunned moment then she reached for the phone on the wall and dialed.

"Did you check Zepher?" she said without preamble. She was quiet for a moment. "When is he supposed to be back?" There was a pause. "Check his place, now. Call me back after you do. And don't go alone. Get everyone else in the building."

She hung up the phone and looked at Tink.

"Bull's funeral is today. Out of town. Zepher left last night and isn't due back until tomorrow. What's going on, Tink?"

Ambrey clutched her towel, her knuckles white. Water dripped from her hair to the floor as we waited for her to say something.

I set my hands on her shoulders and carefully drew her back against me. A tremble ran through her.

"Talk to us," I said softly.

"Rogan, I need to think." Her tone carried a hint of reprimand.

Shay's questioning gaze met mine. I shrugged. I was clueless what was going through Ambrey's mind but knew when she was ready to share, she would.

After a moment, Shay went down the hall and disappeared into a room. She came back a moment later with a fluffy lavender robe.

Silently, she handed it to me. I covered Ambry and pulled her wet hair off her shoulders. Ambrey pulled away from me and threaded her arms through the sleeves as she went to the window.

"When will the rain stop?" she asked.

"It's supposed to go all day," Shay said.

"We can't wait. It will only get worse."

"What will?" I asked.

She turned to look at me, twin spots of color slowly expanding on her cheeks.

"Your ex's temper," she said.

My gut clenched.

"It was Arya?" Shock robbed my voice of volume. I looked around the room at the human friends I'd made. Weak and powerless. Arya would kill them all. Not to get to me, but because she was that far gone to the descent.

"I need to get dressed," Ambrey said, moving toward the still open door. "As soon as the kids are done eating, come upstairs. You're too close to the entrance."

I followed Ambrey to our apartment. She went straight to the window to check the street. I stood behind her, staring out into the rain.

"We can't wait for Arya to show herself again," she said softly. "We need to find her before she hurts anyone else."

"I'm sorry." I wasn't usually into self-blame, but no matter how I looked at this, all roads led back to me. I'd brought my troubles and the crazy bitch into their lives.

"Stop it," Ambrey said. "It's not your fault. It's hers."

She turned and pressed another kiss to my lips.

"Get ready," she said when she pulled back. "We're going out."

TINK

I redressed quickly, the wet blouse giving me trouble. While I struggled with the buttons, my mother's lectures and lessons ran through my head.

A female in descent would be overcome with blood urges. Violent and gorging on kills. The blood urges drive us to hunt for small game, then bigger game, until we start to consider humans. The Lutha, to protect our kind, forbade the killing of humans. There were always whispers of humans turning up shredded from some animal attack but as long as the human eye never turned toward the girdack, the Lutha would never search out the female responsible.

As long her daughter disposed of Zepher's body, there was no reason for her mother to punish her. That meant the humans needed to find Zepher.

When I turned to rush out the door, Rogan stood in the opening.

"You'll be cold," he said, considering my wet clothes.

"Yes. Whether I walk out the door in wet clothes or dry, I will be cold. We need to find Zepher's remains before Arya can get rid of him."

Rogan nodded, stepped out of my way, and followed me out of the apartment. Shay was waiting for us at the bottom of the steps.

"They searched his place. It's neat and clean. No sign of anything suspicious."

I was about to nod and move past her when she spoke.

"But Marge, on block seven, called to say his car is parked

in an alley near her place. She saw it rocking and figured he'd found himself a girl."

He had. The wrong girl.

"Thank you, Shay. Get those kids upstairs. Lock the door."

Shay's lips thinned with worry as she moved to let us pass. Before the door closed, I heard her yelling for her nephews, niece, and Denz.

I started jogging toward block seven, and Rogan kept pace beside me. I was grateful for his company.

It took us just minutes to reach the right block, then another few minutes to find the alley. Zepher's rusted-out car was parked as far back as the trash would allow. The windows were fogged from the inside, hiding what we might find.

"Rogan, take a step back," I said.

If Arya was in there, I didn't want him hurt when I opened the door.

Using my sleeve to grip the cold, steel handle, I wiped the water from my face with my other hand then pulled the door open. The hinges protested as I eased the driver's side wide.

Zepher was draped across the front seats, his legs on the driver's side with his headless torso on the passenger side. Blood covered everything. The cloth interior. The dashboard. The floor. His cloths. His skin. Finger trails scored the red as if Arya had painted with it. Chunks of flesh were missing from his arm. For a moment, I could only stare. Without the head, it didn't quite seem like Zepher, the boy I'd watched grow. The boy who'd lost his mother and father in the first few years I'd been here.

Forcing myself to focus, I leaned to the side to try to see his stomach, the choicest place to gorge. The dark, wet glisten of his shirt didn't bode well, and I struggled between pity and anger over what he'd likely suffered before she'd ended it. After a few deep breaths, I resumed studying the interior.

I checked the backseat, closed the door, then checked the rest of the alley. Once I knew it was clear, I turned to Rogan.

"It's him?" he asked softly.

"It is. Come on."

We walked to the end of the alley.

"Go into this building. Knock on the first apartment door and tell Anthony I need him out here."

Rogan didn't question why I was sending him inside instead of going myself. The truth was that I didn't trust that his crazy ex wasn't somewhere close, watching and hoping I'd leave him alone. So, I watched over Zepher's remains and the evidence we needed as Rogan jogged to the building.

He returned a minute later with a short young man who wore his pants far too low, considering the belt around his hips.

"What did I tell you about your underwear?" I said.

"Sorry, Tink." He quickly pulled up his pants and tightened the belt. "I was—"

"I don't care. You were warned once already." Fear crept into his eyes. "Tomorrow, come by my place. I'll give you enough money for two new pair of pants that fit. You will give me all the pants you own, or have borrowed, that cannot stay up without a belt. There's a fat man who can use them."

"Yes, Tink."

"Now, I have a hard task for you."

I reached out and set a hand on his shoulder. His activities that day flashed in my mind. I saw the woman he'd just left, and the man he'd met afterward for the pot he was nervously hiding in his baggy pants. My frustration spiked, and my fingers bit into his shoulders.

He flinched slightly but didn't try to leave. He knew better.

"Anthony, go to the car and open the door. Look at everything. Then go inside and call the police."

"Police?"

"Yes. Police. We'll wait across the hall with Marge until after they've left."

"Uh...Tink? There's something I should—"

"I suggest you flush what's in your pocket and give Marge your contaminated pants. Just in case."

He paled and said a soft, "yes, Tink," before starting down the alley. Rogan watched him for a moment before speaking.

"Ambrey, what are you—"

"She painted with his blood and was eating on him. It's clear this wasn't an animal kill." I glanced at Rogan. "The Lutha can't ignore the publicity this kind of kill will bring. She'll be forced to call her daughter home to deal with her."

The groan of metal on metal drew my attention. I watched Anthony look inside, turn, and throw up all over the pavement. When he was done, he straightened and looked inside again. He gagged but didn't throw up before closing the door and coming our way.

"Is that Zepher?" His voice shook just as hard as his

33

hands. Some of my annoyance with him faded. I cared for everyone in my community. Even those who sometimes strayed from the rules.

"You have a phone call to make," I said instead of answering. If I told him it was Zepher, the police would want to know how he knew.

He swallowed hard and looked up into the rain. I could still smell the vomit on him and knew he was struggling not to do so again. Yet, we didn't have the time to let him recover. My back still itched, and I felt certain Arya was still out there, somewhere, waiting.

"Anthony," I said, sternly.

"Yeah. I know. I got a call to make. What should I say?"

"How about you took out the garbage and saw a car you thought you recognized?"

"And looked inside," he finished with a sigh.

"And wished you hadn't," Rogan said.

"You got that right."

We left the mouth of the alley and walked toward the apartment, passing Marge's front window. She had the curtains partially opened, and I saw her sitting in her living room chair. From her apartment, we would be able to watch the alley. Marge had her door open when we stepped inside.

I slipped off my coat and shook the water from it as Anthony kept going toward his apartment.

"Are you all right?" Rogan asked softly.

"Yes and no," I said. "You and I are not strangers to violence, but they are. At least, to the level that's coming our way if we don't stop her."

Rogan ran a hand through his wet hair and opened his mouth to say more, but Marge interrupted.

"Do you want a towel?" she called from her apartment.

I walked toward her door.

"Yes, please. But stay sitting and keep watch on the alley. I'll get the towel," I said.

She immediately stood.

"I have a better view of the alley from the other chair," she explained as she hobbled to the chair near the window. "What am I watching for?"

"Anyone not a police officer."

"Towels are in the bathroom on the top shelf in the linen closet."

Rogan stayed in the doorway while I got us towels. I handed him one and used the other to attempt to dry my hair.

"Can we stay with you for a while?" I asked.

"Of course," she said, not taking her eyes from the window.

Rogan stepped in and closed the door. We stood in silence for several minutes.

"Did you two eat, yet?" she asked as sirens wailed in the distance.

"No, ma'am," Rogan said.

"Go fix us some sandwiches. It's about time Tink accepted my invitation for lunch."

With Marge's view of the alley, it was likely the police would have questions for her. Yet, Rogan and I couldn't leave. And, she knew we would need a reason to be there.

We all had plates with a sandwich and chips when an

officer knocked on Marge's door.

Four

ROGAN

Since we'd returned from Marge's, Ambrey had said very little as she paced the living room of her apartment. It could have been that Zepher's death was still tormenting her. She had an undeniably deep connection with her community. But, she didn't smell or look sad.

Keeping quiet, I stirred the chili that Shay had simmering on the stove and continued to watch and wait for a sign that Ambrey needed me.

I wasn't the only one unsure of her mood. Will, Denz, and Shay sat on the sofa with Kye and Calem on the floor near their feet.

"Should we go back to our place, Tink?" Shay asked.

"No. Not yet. My back still itches," Ambrey said without pausing her steps.

I caught the look that Kye shot Shay.

"Kye, contain your sass," Ambrey said, sharply.

Kye's eyes rounded and her bottom lip started to quiver.

"Shay, would you mind taking everyone to Cara's? She's not working tonight," I said.

When Ambrey didn't say anything against the idea, the family was quick to leave and close the door behind them.

I stayed in the kitchen, watching Ambrey's prowling moves. She was tense and on edge. Her blouse had dried as had her skirt. My librarian was rumpled. Stern and rumpled. A sassy combination. Perverse or not, I couldn't help wanting her right then.

Her movements stopped. Rigid, she stood facing the window and inhaled deeply.

"Rogan," she said. "Not now."

Her words were a no, but the tone wasn't. She needed me but didn't want to. Not now, when she thought her community was in danger.

I shut off the burner and started toward the bedroom, letting my mind wander to all the naughty things we could do together...if she joined me. Her pacing stopped, and a soft growl followed me down the hall. I smiled as I quickly stripped, already anticipating what would come.

Before I could turn, her nails raked my skin, followed by her tongue. I hissed out a breath at the pain and pleasure.

"Don't say no." Her hands smoothed over my ribs and stomach, then lower.

I groaned when she held me tightly.

"Say yes," she demanded. "Say you're mine."

"Yes. I'm yours."

She turned me and threw me onto the bed.

"Mine. Not Arya's."

It took an hour before Ambrey fell into the mattress beside me. My chest heaved with each breath. I'd given her everything she'd demanded and had unapologetically enjoyed every moment of it.

"It's not getting better," she said.

"What isn't?" I asked, wiping a hand down her sweaty back.

"The burning that's right between my shoulder blades. It's getting worse. It started before we knew about Zepher, and it keeps getting stronger. Something is still wrong. Until I know Arya is no longer out there, no one is safe."

"The police are out there, investigating and following leads. Your people are smart. They will follow your rules and stay safe."

She turned her head to meet my gaze.

"For how long?"

I had no answer for her. She was right. Until the Lutha learned of her daughter's killing, there was no guarantee the community would be safe. Even then, who could say the Lutha would call her bitch home. Perhaps Zepher's murder was a sanctioned killing, an act to strike fear into the community. If that was the case, our hell was only beginning.

"Yes," Ambrey said, cringing as if I'd spoken my thought aloud. "We need to contact the Lutha. My parents live in one of the outlying communities. It would take them time to reach the Lutha. You were chosen, which means your family is closer."

She wanted me to reach out to my parents.

"They won't talk to me. According to Cael, my mother said I was a disgrace. She won't recognize me if I call."

"If you tell her you're mated, she may listen."

"No, she'll question. She'll want to know what challenges you've won."

"Rogan, I need you to try. Make the call."

I rubbed a hand over my face then sat up.

"Thank you, Rogan."

"Don't thank me yet. We may not like what we hear."

I tugged on the spare pair of jeans and a clean shirt Ambrey had secured for me then left the bedroom. When I opened the apartment door, I found Denz sitting on the floor in the hallway.

He stood quickly at the sight of me.

"Hey, Shay wants to know if we can go back downstairs."

"No. But, can I use your phone?"

"Sure."

He went back to Cara's place while I jogged downstairs and let myself into their apartment. I stared at the wall phone for a moment. How long had it been since I last spoke to my parents? Months. Before Ambrey, I'd obsessed over the idea of going home and seeing them again. However, the echo of Cael's words robbed me of any anticipation as I picked up the phone.

I listened to the line ring twice before my mother picked up with a friendly greeting. My chest tightened at the sound of her voice.

"Mom, don't hang up. I'm mated and need to reach the Lutha."

There was a moment of silence.

"Mated?"

"Yes. Her name is Ambrey. I was running from Cael, and

she stepped in. She's perfect, Mom."

"You went against the Lutha, and you want me to what? Rub it in her face?"

"She already knows, Mom.   Cael came here and challenged me after the mating. I won."

"You won?" Her voice had dropped to an awed whisper.

"Yeah. But, Ayra's here. She's killed her first human and left evidence where it was found. The Lutha needs to do something before we're all exposed."

"Tell me about her. Your mate."

"And the Lutha?"

"I'll go to her after we're done speaking."

TINK

I stood in the hall, listening to Rogan speak to his mother.

"Her name is Ambrey, and she's amazing. She's not like any other female I've met. She's strong, but she doesn't flaunt it. And she dresses in prim cloths that drive me crazy."

I smiled slightly and looked down at my blouse and skirt. They were a disguise, necessary to beguile humans. He was right about me not flaunting my powers. I couldn't. Not here in the human world. Even in these clothes, I made most humans nervous.

"She looks like a sexy librarian and acts it, too. She's kind of quiet and really smart."

Heat flooded my cheeks at his praise.

"I can't really talk about that, Mom. Just know that I like where I am and who I'm with." He was quiet for a moment then told his mother he loved her too and hung up.

I moved to stand in the doorway so he would see me when he turned. He didn't seem surprised at my presence and walked toward me with a half-smile curving his lips.

"Do you think she'll speak to the Lutha?" I asked.

"Yes. My mother has no fear." His smile faded.

"And that worries you?"

"The outcome of their talk worries me."

I laced my fingers through his, allowing his worries to become my own. The Lutha could kill his mother for stepping forward to announce her daughter's actions or because she had spoken to her son after he'd rejected the Lutha's daughter. The scenarios running through his mind made my head hurt.

"Stop, Rogan."

I pulled him down for a kiss, determined not to ease up until his thoughts focused on only me. However, the taste of him on my lips ignited my hunger and the kiss turned demanding quickly.

When he tried to pull away, it was too late for me to let him go. I wanted him, again. Too much. Despite the throbbing need pulsing through my body, I realized the danger of the moment and tried to regain a measure of restraint. It wasn't easy when he was so obedient and inviting. I trembled as I struggled not to throw him on the floor.

I wanted to rake my nails over his skin. Devour him. I growled and tried to reign in what I felt, the need to possess and take. Yanking my hands from his hair, I fisted them behind me. With one last swipe of my tongue, I tore my lips from his.

"Go," I said. Rage flared at the idea of letting him walk away, and I brought my fists to my temples fighting my cravings with every bit of will I possessed.

I didn't realize I had my eyes closed until I felt his lips brush against mine. Need ripped at me.

"Don't fight what you feel, Ambrey. I am yours. Any time you need me."

His hands brushed over mine.

"I am yours," he repeated in a whisper. His fingers trailed down the front of my shirt, making me pant and shake until his hands wrapped around my waist. With an aggressive hold, he pressed his hips into mine, showing me just how much he wanted to be mine.

I lost control. With a feral snarl, I grabbed his head and kissed him hard. His fingers tangled in my hair, and his tongue met mine.

Everything after that was a blur of flying clothes and sweaty skin. We didn't stop until the pressure in my head eased.

Collapsing on top of him, I idly licked the sweat on his skin, just for a taste, then sighed. The intensity was gone, but I could feel it lingering just beneath the surface.

"What is happening to me?"

He leaned forward and kissed my temple before letting his head fall back to the carpet.

"Since I've never been mated before, I can't say. But,"— he swatted my bare butt—"I like it."

Although his words were sweet, I wasn't reassured. He shifted under me.

"We should probably get off Shay's floor before someone comes looking for us. I didn't manage to completely close the door."

Moving off of him, I grabbed my clothes and quickly redressed while considering what had just happened. The urges and the unease were getting worse. I couldn't run a community if I spent half my time in the bedroom—or on the carpet—with Rogan.

Frustrated with my lack of control and the location in which I'd lost it, I walked back upstairs. Rogan went to invite Shay's family and Cara to eat dinner with us while I started setting out bowls. The meal passed quickly, and everyone seemed more relaxed.

Before we had to talk about where everyone would sleep, because I still didn't like the idea of them at street level, the phone downstairs rang.

I went with Shay to answer it.

"Hello?" She glanced at me as she listened. "He's not here right now..."

I held out my hand before she finished the thought, and she passed the phone without a word to the caller.

"This is Ambrey," I said.

"Ambrey, this is Cathan, Rogan's mother. The Lutha has called Arya home." The news didn't ease the itch plaguing me, and her next words explained why. "And you've both been summoned."

"Summoned?"

"You have two days to arrive." She paused for a moment. "Please come," she added softly.

I could hear the fear in her words. If we didn't come, would something happen to Rogan's family? Given how he felt about his mother, I couldn't ignore the Lutha's request.

"We will see you soon."

After I hung up, I turned to Shay.

"You can come back down here. But stay alert. Keep the community alert. Rogan and I will need to leave in the morning." I started toward the door.

"When will you be back?"

I paused and looked steadily into the eyes of the woman I had known for years. It had taken me so long to know these people and gain their understanding. They were a part of me. And leaving now, even to protect everyone, felt like I was abandoning them.

"I don't know."

Rogan waited at the apartment door. His gaze swept my face as he stepped aside to let us in. I could feel his curiosity, but he didn't ask questions until Shay took her kids downstairs. I joined him in the kitchen as he was putting away the bowls.

"What did Mom say?" he asked.

I grabbed the washcloth from the sink.

"The Lutha called her daughter home, but she summoned us as well."

"What for?"

"Your mother didn't say, and I don't think the reason would change the answer. We have to go." I finished wiping down the counter. It was odd not reaching for the bleach.

"When do we leave?"

I turned and found him leaning against the fridge, watching me.

"Tomorrow morning, first thing."

Rogan moved toward me and set his hands on my shoulders.

"Before you, I dreamt of going home. Now, I know I'm already home, and I don't want to leave. I can't tell you everything will be okay. When dealing with the Lutha, nothing is certain. But we'll be together."

I wrapped my arms around his waist and leaned into him.

"Together," I said softly.

Five

TINK

I impatiently shifted in my seat. The feeling of unrest still prickled along my spine, but that wasn't the main problem at the moment. I needed Rogan again. Under me. Over me. Touching me. Filling me.

"Do you want me to stop?" Rogan asked, glancing at me, unaware.

"No." I wanted to reach our destination, face the Lutha, and go home where I could fully give into my urges.

The thought of willingly walking back into the girdack world turned my stomach sour. There were no pleasant memories for me to revisit, only countless hours of training and lessons and fights. Fights that I had purposely lost to avoid further challenges. Lessons that I'd memorized as quickly as possible to avoid hearing the same thing again and again. However, there had been no avoiding training. Not when I'd lost so many challenges. In an effort to improve me, my mother had handed me my ass over and over again.

I thought of Shay and Kye. They'd taught me more about what a mother-daughter relationship should be like than my own parents. Smiles. Laughter. Unity.

"Ambrey, ease up, sweetheart," Rogan said with a sideways glance at the seat.

I followed his gaze.

"Shay's car isn't the best, but she's not going to appreciate rips in the seats."

My claws had come out. Long and lethal. I held them up and looked at them.

"It's been years since they've come out," I said. "Since before I left home."

Was it thinking of home that had brought them back? The spiders continued to burrow into my brain, and the tingle continued to burn my back. No, it wasn't my thoughts. My control was slipping.

I focused on the texture and shape of the nails I wanted. Harmless. Human. Slowly, the nails shifted back into a safer form.

Rogan reached over and gave my hand a light squeeze. The gesture of comfort wrapped around me. Had I ever been soothed like that? I couldn't ever remember my mother comforting me. My father had remained quietly uninvolved, largely due to my mother's influence. Once I'd left, I'd found the humans standoffish. I'd tried to blend, to be less intimidating, but it had only gotten me so far. The humans in the community were respectfully aware of me.

Rogan continued to be my first true source of solace in years. I stared forward and resisted the urge to lean over and lick him.

We traveled most of the day and pulled into the driveway of his parents' home close to dinner. I took in the area where

Rogan had grown up with mild curiosity. The house was neatly cared for, and there was a duck shaped mailbox at the end of the drive. Cute and homey, as were the rest of the houses. Very different from the neighborhood I'd known in my youth. The wooded subdivision made a perfect location for a community of werewolves, and I wished I'd grown up in this community.

Before Rogan had the car parked, the front door opened. A tall woman with Rogan's dark hair stood in the opening, watching us. Cathan. His mother.

She wore an air of confident dominance, easy to spot in our females. I hoped she wouldn't try to challenge me to test my worthiness. Not that I'd blame her. Her son would have been mate to the next Lutha if not for my interference.

Rogan glanced at me, his face a mask of nervous anticipation. Memories of his mother's hugs and kisses wrapped around my mind. His childhood had been completely different from mine. Rogan's mother loved him very much. And he loved her. I hoped that would be enough to smooth things over.

He and I left the car and approached the house.

Cathan's cool gaze swept over me as I neared.

"Mother," Rogan said. "This is Ambrey."

He set his arm possessively around my waist, and I fought the urge to lean into him. I couldn't afford to show any weakness until we knew the reason for our summons.

"Ambrey, you look unimposing and unworthy of my son."

Rogan tensed beside me and his thoughts were easy to read. He was worried I would hurt his mother.

ROGAN

"A good mother will always think that," Ambrey said calmly.

My mother, the woman I hadn't seen for months, continued to stare at my mate. The challenge in her eyes was unmistakable as was her soft growl.

"We're here to answer the summons," Ambrey said, ignoring the challenge.

My mother frowned at Ambrey.

"How long have you been hiding among the humans that you don't remember—"

"I remember very well," Ambrey said. "There is no point to accepting your challenge. I am not a member of the girdack. Winning will give you no honor or elevation. Now, will you invite us in to meet your mate? He's worrying you will chase away your son."

Mother's eyes rounded a bit before she frowned at Ambrey. Did she now understand how special Ambrey was? I hoped so.

"Come in." She moved aside and led Ambrey into the house. The homey living room hadn't changed since I'd left.

My father stood in the middle of the room, an anxious gaze on his face. His light brown hair was longer since I'd last seen him, and a scruff of beard coated his jaw. But, the way his eyes creased when he smiled at me was the same.

I left Ambrey to give my father a long hug.

"We've missed you," he said quietly, holding me tightly.

"I've missed you, too."

He clapped my back then pulled away to look at me.

"You're hungry," he said, looking into my eyes. "Let's go cook."

I hesitated to follow when he gave me a tug toward the kitchen.

"Ambrey," my mother said, "please have a seat. Rogan, go with your father."

Ambrey nodded when I looked her way. I didn't like leaving her alone with my mother. Not after her attempt to challenge Ambrey.

My mother gave me an arched, impatient stare, and I went to the kitchen with Dad. His expression conveyed his sympathy while we silently started preparing dinner. Mother loved me, but when it came to protecting me, she was a little overbearing. Not that I blamed her after everything the Lutha had tried to do and, probably, still wanted to do. My mom would find out soon enough just how amazing Ambrey was.

"Have you spoken with the Lutha?" Ambrey asked from the living room.

Dad winked at me as we listened to their conversation.

"Not since the summons."

"No reason was provided?"

"No."

After that, they remained quiet.

"She's pretty," Dad said softly as he handed me two onions.

"She's...everything," I said, unable to put into words how much Ambrey meant to me. Dad flashed me a knowing smile and went back to making burger patties. Knowing that he understood helped me not worry as much about the continued silence in the living room.

After we'd fried up a dozen burgers, we set everything out on the kitchen table. Before Dad could tell Mom the meal was ready, we heard her phone chirp.

"Hello?" She said nothing for several seconds before adding, "I understand."

Dad and I exchanged a look. Mom didn't usually answer the phone so formally. When nothing else was spoken, we knew the call had ended. He moved to the doorway, and I waited by the table in anticipation as he told Mom and Ambrey the food was ready.

Ambrey and I had been apart for what? Thirty minutes? Yet, the need to see her, touch her, taste her, and please her teased the back of my mind. Ambrey was under my skin and in my blood.

The women joined us in the kitchen. Dad sat across from me with Ambrey to my right and Mother to my left at the circular table.

"I'm Ross," Rogan's father said to Ambrey as he passed me the ketchup. "How long have you been mated?"

"Three days."

Dad's mouth dropped opened a little as he glanced back and forth between me and Ambrey. Mom made a noise of disbelief, and Ambrey flushed. I didn't know if it was due to anger or embarrassment until she spoke.

"Yes. Sitting here is exceedingly difficult," Ambrey said, looking at my Mom.

"How long will it take to reach the Lutha from here?"

Ambrey asked.

"An hour."

"We'll leave after dinner."

Ambrey began eating her burger, but my parents still hadn't moved.

"There's a girdack meeting tomorrow morning. She'll receive you then," Mother said with just a hint of uncertainty in her tone. The only time I'd heard that was just before I'd run from the Lutha and Arya.

Ambrey paused mid-chew, her head jerking slightly. Her gaze locked onto the table, and the slow curl of fingers crushed her food. She set her mangled burger on her plate and brought her fists up to her head, pressing them into her temples like she had in Shay's apartment.

"Ambrey," I said softly, reaching for her.

"Don't." She held out her hand to stop me, but her tone had already done that. I could understand her anger. I didn't want to be here any longer than necessary, either.

"Ross, come here please," my mother said, pulling my attention from Ambrey. Mom watched Ambrey with wary calculation while Dad's face was slowly losing color.

"What's wrong?" I asked.

"They're afraid of me, Rogan," Ambrey said.

"Not afraid. Concerned and in shock. There's a reason newly mated pairs aren't seen for days," Mother said, her eyes never leaving Ambrey.

"What do you mean?" I asked.

"We usually have no control. We don't want anyone near our male. We need to possess and mark and mate until our scent is in his every pore. Until we're certain we own him."

"Own?" That brought me right back to the feelings I had while running from Arya.

"No, Rogan," Ambrey said. "I don't want to own you."

There was a growl in her voice, a soft warning laced with interest that made me doubt her. And, the idea of being owned, possessed by Ambrey, didn't bother me as much as it should have. Instead, it made my groin tighten.

Her head jerked up and her eyes flashed with an intense light. She'd made the same moves when she'd snapped at Kye. Why she'd become increasingly agitated each time we'd left the bedroom now made more sense.

"So what you're saying, Mother, is that Ambrey and I might want to spend our time in the bedroom while we wait?"

"That would be best for everyone," Mother said.

"We would very much appreciate a room, then," Ambrey said, still holding my gaze. Her intensity exciting me.

"And, Ambrey?" my mother said quietly.

"Yes?"

"We'll leave food outside the door and knock when it's time to leave."

"Thank you," Ambrey said. "Show me your room, Rogan."

Blood rushed south and my jeans tightened painfully at the thought of what I was in for.

TINK

Rogan wasn't helping. Every image in his head was driving my need for him higher. He radiated anticipation as I followed him down the stairs to his lower level bedroom. Barely seeing the twin bed or the empty walls, I closed the door behind us. He turned to face me and unbuttoned his shirt. The breadth of his shoulders made me ache as he shrugged the material away. Then, he stepped toward me.

I closed my eyes and swallowed hard at the almost angry, aggressive wave that prodded me to go to him, to make him mine. There was nothing nice about me. Nothing sexy and smart in that moment. I wanted to take and make a point, like I had with Bull. Rogan was mine. And I hated that I needed to bring him to a girdack meeting. All those females looking at him, thinking about touching him.

Something brushed against the knuckles of my hand, and I realized I once again had them fisted at my temples.

"I'm yours," Rogan whispered.

The horse rasp of his seductive voice wrapped around me. My breathing grew harsher. He fingers trailed over the material covering my forearms. I shivered at the contact.

"Turn around for me," he said. "Let me show you."

I opened my eyes and looked up at him.

"No." The severity of my tone echoed in the almost barren room.

"Tink, look at your hands." The use of my other name shocked me enough that I did as he'd asked. My claws were back. Long and lethal.

"Turn around, Ambrey. I'll help make this better. I swear."

Instinct surged. The need to reach for him consumed me.

"You'll hurt me, Ambrey."

His quiet admission stopped me. He was my lifeline. My link to sanity. I couldn't hurt him. Ever.

I turned and placed my hands flat against the door.

He didn't tease me by undressing me slowly. He bunched my skirt over my hips, ripped my underwear away, and nudged my legs apart. A hiss of impatience still escaped me. I needed him.

My fingers curled against the wood, and I growled a warning. A moment later, he thrust into me, pushing me into the door. I yowled at the sensation, and at the smell of his lust. He grabbed my wrists and held me to the door, crushing into me again and again. He wasn't nice, and it was exactly what I needed. He didn't stop until I'd blissfully screamed his name the third time.

"Are you ready for the bed?" he asked, not withdrawing.

I lifted my cheek from the door and blinked at my hands. The nails were safe again.

"Yes. The bed."

Even knowing he wasn't leaving me, a growl escaped me as he withdrew. When I turned, he was already on the bed.

"Yours," he repeated. I climbed onto him, slowly lowering myself. He groaned and closed his eyes. I gently kissed his lips, and he wrapped his hands around my hips.

"Mine," I said.

I licked the sweat from his skin and set our pace.

* * * *

I opened my eyes and yawned. Morning light was creeping through the high window, an indication of the time Rogan and I had passed in his room. It felt like we'd only just fallen asleep. Likely, we had.

I breathed in the scent of his dried sweat, so close to my nose. Sleeping in a twin with Rogan, meant that I slept on Rogan. And I loved it. Although that nagging feeling was still twitching the skin on my back, I didn't feel so restless anymore. I'd always thought my mother's lessons about being newly mated were over dramatic. Why wouldn't I be able to control myself with my mate? Yet, Cathan seemed to hold the same beliefs, given her reaction last night. I wondered what she would have done in my situation. Ignore my responsibilities to my community and the Lutha's summons just for sex. Amazing, wonderful sex.

My stomach growled, but I wasn't ready to get out of bed yet. True to her word, Rogan's mother had kept a supply of food outside the door for Rogan to retrieve every time he had opened it. I lifted my head to see if there was something to eat close by. Instead, my gaze fell on the door. Furrows scored the right and left sides, head high. I frowned. Twice in the same day I'd lost control of my hands. Losing control was unacceptable. However, now that I was thinking more clearly, something else disturbed me besides the persistent tingle along my spine.

The claws shouldn't have happened so easily, no matter my control.

Setting my head back on Rogan's chest, I studied the

furrows and thought back to my lessons and training. Two types of challenges occurred at two different times in lunar cycle. When the moon was full, challenges to settle disputes were conducted in our fully shifted forms. When the moon became new, we fought in our human forms to determine our hierarchy, male and female. Fighting still occured in between, but I could only ever remember human forms. Never partial shifts. Why then, in all the lessons I'd committed to memory, couldn't I recall any rules about not shifting during other times in the lunar cycle?

"Good morning," Rogan rumbled beneath me.

I stilled, realizing I'd been tracing his closest nipple with my finger.

"Good morning."

"Are you hungry? I think there's a sandwich left." He shifted slightly beneath me. I licked his nipple, then nipped it.

"Or if you'd rather do something else..." He gripped my waist and seated me more firmly on his hips. The manic obsessive need from yesterday had abated, but I still craved him in a way that wouldn't let me go.

"Once more," I said, raking my nails along his sides. "And then we'll join your parents for breakfast."

I claimed his lips in an affectionate kiss and set aside my thoughts about control for another hour.

Six

Listening to the shower run, I stood slowly. Everything was sore, especially my cock. The mirror on the back of the bathroom door, which had given me amazing views while the two of us were in bed, now displayed every bruise and welt on my skin. I didn't mind them. Ambrey had been so out of control last night, it was lucky I hadn't suffered worse. But, I knew if I didn't cover up before she was done, she would mind them. I slipped into my jeans and gently adjusted the well-used appendage.

My mother's words rang in my mind, and I wondered how any males before me had managed a week straight of what Ambrey and I had done in the last few hours. Honestly, I'd loved every intense moment of our bed play. Ambrey needed me, and every time we were together proved how much. However, her desperation when we'd first come into this room made me very aware of my mistake. She needed me at regular intervals. Waiting too long was dangerous for both of us.

The water turned off just as I tugged a shirt over my head. Ambrey walked out, wrapped in a towel, and stopped at the sight of me.

"Aren't you showering?"

"And wash away the smell of you? Not a chance. I worked hard to smell like this."

She gave me a small smile and went to the bag I'd found outside our door. She put on her bra and picked up the matching panties.

"Leave those," I said. Who knew how long we'd need to wait for the Lutha to appear once the girdack gathered. It would be easier to scratch her itch if there was nothing under her skirt. The image of her pressed against the door as I took her from behind drifted through my mind, and I started to harden, which wasn't yet a pleasant feeling. Concentrating, I imagined Cael kicking my ass the moment before I met Ambrey. It helped settle things down.

Ambrey gave me a curious look, but set the panties aside and finished dressing without them.

We went upstairs and found my parents in the kitchen. Mother noticed us first and stopped chopping onions to study Ambrey.

"Good morning, Cathan, Ross. Can we help?"

Dad stopped cracking eggs and turned to look at Ambrey then me.

"No," he said, drawing out the word with uncertainty.

"There's still time before we need to leave," Mother said. "If you want to go back and..."

I subtly shook my head behind Ambrey's back, desperate not to be sent to my room again.

Ambrey sighed and glanced over her shoulder at me. I

did my best to look innocent.

"We're ready to take a small break," she said, facing my Mother.

Mom looked at Ambrey with a bit of awe and respect.

"A break? Ambrey, no one takes a break in the first five days. Your control is remarkable."

"Not very. I'm afraid I've damaged Rogan's door."

"No worries," Dad said, seeming to shake off his shock. "I've repaired my share of doors. Hope you're hungry."

"Not with that image in my head," I grumbled as I sat at the table.

Mom flicked my ear as she passed me. A deep warning growl rumbled from Ambrey. Mom quickly drew back and I set my hand on Ambrey's arm.

"I deserved that," I said softly.

Ambrey took a slow breath then apologized to Mom, breaking the tension. My parents hurried to serve us breakfast, and as soon as we finished, we left the house.

The drive to the girdack took an hour just as Mom had said, but by the time we reached the dirt road outside of Eureka Springs, Ambrey was already on edge again. The industrial building that the Lutha owned and maintained for meetings was a few minutes further, and tucked into the wooded hills at the dead end, it provided a private place for girdack business.

Ours wasn't the first car to arrive. No one spoke as we exited the vehicle and followed other attendees across the gravel parking lot. Another male held the door for us as we entered the steel roofed building.

Inside, many others already mingled in the center of the cavernous space. The hushed tones echoed softly. No one paid us attention. The focus remained on the opposite end of the large building, where a platform had been built. One chair, ornate and carved like an old king's throne, sat on a second platform stacked on the first. While the rest of us stood, the Lutha would sit and look over us. There would be no hiding in the crowd from her watchful eyes.

As Ambrey's gaze remained locked on the throne, more tension crept into her shoulders.

"We'll join you in a moment, Mother," I said as I took Ambrey's hand.

She followed me and didn't question when I tugged her into the men's bathroom. As I'd guessed, it was empty. I picked a stall and closed us in. When I turned, she pulled me down to her lips and kissed me gently. My jeans grew uncomfortably tight before she pulled away.

"Rogan, I know you're sore," she said. "I'm still fine."

"I know you are. That's exactly why I pulled you in here. Better to take care of things before they get..."

"Crazy?"

"Dangerous for the doors."

Her lips twitched.

"I don't think I'm ready to sacrifice you for a door," she said, gently cupping my groin. It made the ache worse, a combination of good and bad.

"Perhaps there's something else I can do to help." I knelt before her and slid my hands up along the outside of her legs. Her skirt slowly lifted, and her breathing quickened.

"Could you hold onto the bars for me?" I asked once her skirt was around her waist. "I don't want to lose hair."

She gripped the bars on either side of her, and I wrapped my hand around the back of her right leg, just behind the knee. I lifted it up and set it over my shoulder.

"Remember to be quiet," I said, leaning forward.

TINK

I gripped the bars and held my tongue while Rogan wielded his. The raw animalistic force I'd been struggling to hold back boiled forth. I threw my head back and let go of everything except the bars. My release was quick and strong, and the steel under my palms groaned. When the last of my tremors ceased, he set my leg back to the floor and straightened my skirt.

"Better?" he asked, standing, his boyish smile full of pride.

I swallowed hard and nodded, willing myself to loosen my hold on the steel. When I did, his gaze flicked to the damage.

"I'm really glad that wasn't my head."

"Me too. Let's go and find out what the Lutha wants from us."

The room had filled noticeably by the time we emerged from the bathroom. Rogan's father, who'd been just outside the door, nodded to us. His consideration to guard the door and ensure our privacy made me grateful.

We followed him further into the room and stopped beside Cathan. Groups gathered, conversing in normal volumes that collectively created a din. I caught words here and there, most speculating why a meeting had been called.

"Mostly community leaders," Cathan said softly for my benefit. "A few strong females being groomed to take over leadership roles."

"No Lutha?" I asked.

Cathan shook her head.

"Ambrey?" a voice called out.

A ball tightened in my stomach at the sound, and I turned toward the source rushing toward me. The tall and lithe woman was dressed in hip hugging jeans with sturdy boots and a shirt that said, "Bitch, please." I looked at the same blonde hair and oval face as mine.

"Ambrey," my mother said again. "It is you." She wrapped me in a tight, brief hug.

"I'm glad you came to your senses," she continued as she stepped back. Her brown eyes swept over me, head to toe.

"What are you wearing? We'll need to find you something else before we go home. No one will take any challenge you issue seriously if you're dressed like that."

Beyond having more grey in her hair, she hadn't changed at all. I'd thought I would feel the same overwhelming need to escape I'd felt just before I'd left home. Instead, I felt very little for her, except mild annoyance.

"Mother," I said. "This is Cathan, Ross, and Rogan. This is my mother, Eada."

"Hello," my mother said, barely sparing them a glance.

Cathan's eyes narrowed, but after a glance at me, she remained quiet.

"How many challenges have you engaged in since you've

been gone? How many did you win?" my mother asked, completely unaware she'd just snubbed an equal.

Rogan made a small noise of amusement, and my mother gave him a harsh look. A rolling wave of defensive aggression tightened my chest. No one scolded Rogan but me. Rogan winked at me, calming me enough to answer her.

"I haven't had to resort to challenges in a while," I said.

"Resort? Challenges are not something we resort to, Ambrey. They control and bring us power. Speaking of power, have you heard that the Lutha's top females are here today? I've heard that her daughter, Arya, might even make an appearance with the Lutha."

"Do you know why we're meeting?" I asked.

It troubled me that the Lutha was gathering her strongest females. A display of power could mean the Lutha wanted to intimidate us. Or she could mean to do something worse. I glanced at Rogan with worry.

"Focus, Ambrey," my mother said sharply, then lowered her voice. "I heard some senseless female challenged Arya for her right to her chosen male."

Cathan sucked in a surprised breath, but I didn't pay my mother's choice of words or Cathan's reaction much attention.

"So today is to witness a challenge?" I asked. The tingle along my spine increased as I took in the size of the crowd now inside the building.

"No. I think there's more than that happening. A challenge like that would have taken place immediately." She turned her attention fully to Rogan again, and I felt my irritation rise.

"You don't look like much of a mate. Rogan, is it? How did you two meet?" she asked.

I should have known she knew he was mine. Rogan looked surprised, though.

"How did you—"

She waved away Rogan's words.

"I have a nose, and her scent is all over you. Could you be any more obvious?"

Rogan shamelessly grinned.

"We can talk more later. Find me after the meeting," Mother said, looking at me once again. "We need to discuss the future, and what leadership roles you can still fill at home."

She turned and left us after that.

"Well, I can see where you get your strength from," Cathan said, diplomatically.

"From the moon," I said. "As do we all." I wouldn't give my mother any credit other than she'd made my life hell while with the girdack.

"What about your father?" Rogan asked. "Where is he?"

"Likely at home, in his chair, enjoying his peace." My father deserved every moment of it.

Rogan wrapped an arm around my waist and pulled me close to his side. Just the level of distraction I needed. I allowed myself to lean into him and breathed in his scent mingled with mine.

Suddenly, the persistent irritating sensation that had bothered me since the hospital intensified and spread until even my fingers tingled. Just as quickly as it had grown, it completely disappeared.

A ripple of silence started in the back corner of the room. I turned my head in that direction but couldn't see a thing because of my height. Still, given the way those before me quickly looked to the ground, I knew who was finally making her appearance. The Lutha.

I didn't like that the disquiet I had been feeling since the hospital vanished with her presence. Had what I felt been because of her and not her daughter? The likelihood that it had didn't bode well.

All noise faded. People turned toward the platform at the back of the building and watched for the Lutha to take her place. She ruled the girdack, and her throne was the reminder. However, hers wasn't the first face I saw.

A tall young woman stepped up onto the secondary platform, rising above the crowd enough that I could see her from the knees up. She wore a short tight skirt to show her long bare legs. She moved to stand beside the chair and draped an arm over the back, the pose stretching her skimpy tank top across her ample breasts. The neckline dipped dangerously close to the top of her braless nipples. She twitched slightly, in a restless way, as her cool blue eyes swept the crowd. Anyone could see how close she was to descending fully.

Her gaze continued to search the crowd until she found Rogan. Her lips curved into a triumphant smile, showing her crooked, stained teeth. The teeth that had torn into Zepher. My stomach soured and my temper stretched thin. I pushed all my reactions back and forced myself to focus on the situation. I couldn't afford any missteps this time.

Beside me, Rogan shifted uneasily but didn't remove his arm from around my waist. Images of our deaths, brought about by various tormented methods, flashed through his mind and mine. I placed my hand over his and threaded our fingers together.

A mature woman stepped up onto the platform. Her long dark hair was streaked with white and ran down the length of her back. Her clothes were tamer than her daughter's, the typical snug jeans the women of the girdack seemed to favor and a v-neck t-shirt.

When she turned to sit on her throne, her sharp gaze roved the room. While several other females stepped up onto the platform, similarly dressed and of varying ages, the Lutha's eyes met mine and our gazes held. I didn't look away as I'd been taught to do. I wasn't one of the girdack and owed her nothing. She needed to know, she couldn't control me.

Her growl filled the room.

"It has come to my attention that one of our kind has been living with humans. Let the offender step forward."

In that moment, I understood what the Lutha planned.

Seven

ROGAN

Ambrey released my hand and started forward without hesitation. I followed, watching those around us shuffle aside, backing away as if they too would fall under the Lutha's scrutiny if they came too close. Cowards. All of them. I'd at least had the balls to run when the Lutha tried shoving her crazy-ass daughter at me. Not one of these people had a backbone. Not like Ambrey, who stopped at the base of the platform and met the Lutha's gaze. I stopped two or three feet behind my mate, in clear view of everyone, including Arya whose hungry gaze remained locked on me.

Somewhere in the back of the room, I heard Ambrey's mother gasp. Ambrey's lips twitched. No love lost between her and her mother.

At the sight of Ambrey's half-smile, the Lutha scowled and addressed the girdack.

"We have one unbreakable rule," she said to the room. "Don't talk about the girdack with humans. The punishment is death for the offender, and death to any human with knowledge of the girdack. What do you have to say for yourself?" The Lutha's gaze pinned Ambrey.

Anger had me opening my mouth to hotly deny the claim, but Ambrey spoke first.

"I say it's a false charge to hide the fact your daughter ate a human and left evidence were other humans could find it."

The Lutha's face flushed, and she pulled her teeth back in a silent snarl. Ambrey didn't react to the threat at all, just continued to look forward. I fought not to grin as murmurs of concern broke out behind us. It wasn't just the accusation against Arya, which did cause the she-wolf's narrowed eyes to focus on Ambrey, but Ambrey's complete composure while facing the Lutha.

Arya didn't have the same cool as her mother or my mate.

"Lying whore! I did nothing," the crazed bitch screeched.

The Lutha's hand whipped up in the air, a command for silence.

Arya seethed through clenched teeth. She might be a Lutha in training, but she didn't even try to disregard the current Lutha's command. Weak. A month ago I wouldn't have thought so. Ambrey changed my view on all of it. The Lutha. The girdack. The hierarchy.

"Enough," the Lutha said with a growl. "The human kill was because of his confession. He knew too much about us. The humans have no proof that will lead them here."

I almost shook my head at their conflicting stories. Ambrey didn't hold back; she snorted.

"She says she didn't kill. You say she did, but to protect us. I say your daughter was hungry for flesh because she's already going mad. That was the reason the human died. We both know he knew nothing of the girdack. And, the humans have fingerprints, DNA samples, and surveillance footage of a woman talking to Zepher outside of a convenience store. Arya's face is clearly recognizable."

That surprised me, but I kept my face carefully blank. The police hadn't said anything about that while they questioned us. But Ambrey had a way of knowing things.

"What proof do you have of this?" the Lutha demanded.

Ambrey twitched slightly and rolled her shoulders as if her back was itching again.

"Proof that the humans have proof? With respect, I don't need proof when the humans already have it. And, this wasn't Arya's first kill. I believe Jackson, Mississippi was the first, wasn't it?"

The Lutha's eyes rounded slightly.

"And, she left evidence there, too. Along with her five other kills. Regardless, she needs to stop eating humans before she exposes us all."

While the Lutha remained stunned, Arya's cold blue eyes never left Ambrey's face. As I watched, a slow, calculating smirk spread on her crazy lips.

"So I killed a few humans," she said with a shrug of her thin shoulder. "I'm not the first, and I won't be the last. I'm sure you've been more than tempted, living among them. However, since I don't try to blend with the humans, they will never find me even if they do have a clear image of my face."

The Lutha seemed to come back from her shock and waved Arya to silence again.

"There is still the matter of telling the humans about us,"

the Lutha said.

"We both know that is an empty accusation. The reason for my summons is standing right behind me," Ambrey said.

Everyone's gaze shifted to me.

"You are trying to find a way to be rid of me so Arya can claim the male who ran from her." There were a few snickers from further back in the room. "And, as I'm sure Cael reported, Rogan and I are mated. So, instead of false accusations, let us address the real issue. Arya wants my mate, and I don't plan to give him up. Ever."

I grinned widely, and my recovering appendage shifted slightly in my jeans. I couldn't help it. I loved when Ambrey was cool and commanding like that. The Lutha, however, did not. She growled at both of us, her gaze flicking to my growing bulge.

Ambrey twitched beside me, not liking the Lutha's attention on me.

"You deny the charge. However, I believe you lie. Three days mated, according to Cael," the Lutha said, "and yet here you stand before me. I question if you truly are mated. Any newly mated female would not be here. And if you lie about your mating, you likely lie regarding your discretion."

"Had I known your summons was optional, I would have stayed home and enjoyed further use of my mate." Arya growled at Ambrey's words.

The Lutha remained quiet, studying Ambrey.

"I permitted you to exist among the humans so long as you remained hidden and caused no trouble for the girdack. Even if you have kept your silence about us, stealing a male has caused trouble. You can no longer shun the girdack. You must take your place."

A place with the girdack? Hell no. I glanced at Ambrey and saw a flush begin to dust her cheeks.

TINK

Taking Arya's mate had made the female look weak. Accusing her of killing without control had made her look weaker. Since I'd refuted the Lutha's first accusation with logic, she'd shifted to a secondary plan. She wouldn't give up. She needed to redeem her successor in the eyes of the girdack.

Do not merely attempt dominance. Prove it. Dominance means power.

I struggled to contain my temper and ignore the thought. Clucking my tongue with impatience, something I learned from Shay, I continued to try to extract Rogan and me from a situation quickly spiraling out of control.

"You, yourself, said we only have one unbreakable rule. There's no law that says we cannot exist with humans or a law that says we must live within the girdack. The true purpose of this summons is to take Rogan from me." I looked at Arya. "He ran for a reason. You disgust him. Pick someone else already. There are numerous males who would be interested in what you have to offer."

The crazed bitch's face turned red. She was close to losing control. Her mind was filled with images of tearing me apart and consuming my flesh, taboo even for us. Her aggression trigger my own, and I fisted my hands at my sides.

Stay focused. Stay in control.

I huffed a sigh. My mother would be delighted to know her lessons were still in my head. I, however, was losing patience with all of it. And the scent of Rogan's arousal wasn't helping. The Lutha was right. I would rather be home in my bedroom with my mate. Preferably naked. And sweaty. And licking his skin.

Closing my eyes, I turned my head toward Rogan and inhaled deeply. My mouth watered. My fingers tingled with the need to touch him.

When I opened my eyes and found him watching me warily, reality shattered the illusion.

"Control yourself," I warned him before focusing on the Lutha once more.

The would-be tyrant was now wearing a smirk matching her daughter's.

"Are you saying you want to be exiled from the girdack?" the Lutha asked.

"I'm saying Rogan and I have both embraced our self-exile and wish to return to it. The girdack's power struggles and manipulations hold no interest to either of us."

"Yet, here you are," she said, standing. "Answering my call."

"Here I am reporting an incident that could jeopardize all of us, girdack and exiled."

"An incident we've discussed."

We hadn't. Not really. But I honestly didn't care if Arya

exposed our kind or not. I'd only returned to prevent any further killings.

"Lovely," I said. "Then Rogan and I will be on our way." I turned and took his hand, ready to pull him from the room.

"Do you think we'll let you leave so easily?"

I released Rogan's hand and impatiently faced the Lutha once more. "No. I'm hoping you'll hurry up and acknowledge your real intent, though. I don't like games."

"I do remember that about you. Your mother tried everything to advance your standing in your community. As a child, you did everything possible to avoid challenges and fighting. I wonder if that has changed."

Arya smirked behind her.

"Walk out of here now, alone," the Lutha continued. "And there will be no challenges."

I snorted. Did she really think that I would just abandon Rogan?

She looked up at the crowd again. "Are you here, Ambrey's mother? Step forward and tell us what you think of your child?"

There was a shuffle of noise behind me, and I braced myself for what would come.

Images flitted through my mind. My mother's disappointment in me growing up. My mother's disapproval when I failed a challenge. My mother cooking dinner as she pointed out my weaknesses and where I needed more control. Never had there been a shred of approval.

Now, there was. It rolled off of her as she stepped to my side. And I hated it.

"I think my child is smart. She's made a place for herself in the outside world and survived for six years without a mate."

I fought not to cringe.

"You almost sound proud of that," the Lutha said.

"I am. She had the strength to last six years. Some can't even manage one without succumbing to the descent."

Ayra growled, and the Lutha's lip pulled back in a sneer. The matriarch looked ready to kill my mother on the spot. I rather hoped she would. I could still have a chance, then, of walking away without a fight.

"Surviving in the human world for six years means nothing. She faced nothing. No challenges. No pack runs during a full moon. No males to tempt her."

My mother snorted. "Is that what you've been attempting to do with Arya? You keep her locked away hoping that she can make it a full year without the temptations. No one, temptations or not, has ever lasted six years. And you know what that means."

One of my mother's lessons popped into my head. If you see someone weaker, issue a challenge. Gain in standing. Gain respect and power.

A vivid picture flashed in my mind. Me sitting in the chair on the platform. Rogan standing to my left side. My mother standing to the right.

I'd been gone for six years. Six years without any contact because her ambitions for me had driven me to leave. And here she was, right back at it. Only this time, she wanted me to rule the girdack.

"I don't want that, Mother," I said. The need to lash out at her gripped me. I felt the length of my sharp, hardened claws bite into the palms of my fisted.

Ayra sniggered, and the Lutha smiled.

"See? No drive for power. Six years in the human world hasn't made her strong, it's made her soft and weak."

Rogan snorted quietly, and the Lutha narrowed her eyes at him.

"Do not speak until directed to or I will wipe this floor with your hide."

The remaining hold on my patience snapped.

"You will not touch him," I said, followed with a growl.

Eight

ROGAN

I glanced at Ambrey, unable to believe what I'd heard. Everything she'd said or done since addressing the Lutha had led me to believe she was trying her best to avoid a fight. But, whether purposely or not, Ambrey had just challenged the Lutha.

I tensed as the Lutha turned on Ambrey with a growl of her own. The already quiet room grew completely silent. No one moved.

The time Ambrey had spent resisting the descent made her strong, but the Lutha was older. Experienced. She'd faced more challenges for control of the girdack in her lifetime than any other Lutha before her. She was in her position for a reason.

After seeing the way Ambrey had dealt with Bull, I felt certain she could win a challenge with most any female in the room. Any female but the Lutha.

I watched the older female apprehensively, ready to step forward, not that I would do much good against her.

The anger on the Lutha's face slowly faded, replaced with calculation. My gut knotted with unease, and Ambrey twitched slightly.

"You cannot challenge me," the Lutha said. "You are nothing. Unproven and a waste of my time."

The tension in the room broke with a rush of whispering voices.

"However, since you're in the mood for a challenge…"

"I'll accept the challenge," one of the women on the platform said.

"No," Ambrey said. Her voice carried through the room, silencing murmurs. "I am not part of the girdack. Exiled, I have no place in your hierarchy."

The Lutha's lips pulled back in a silent snarl. Then all emotion cleared from her face, and she turned to look at her daughter. Arya grinned widely.

"Then I challenge you for the right to Rogan, since he was mine to begin with." Arya looked pointedly at me.

Hell, no. The unease in my stomach soured to the point I felt sick. I hated feeling so powerless and that my voice carried no weight here. One word from me on our behalf would likely cause the conflict that Ambrey was struggling to avoid.

I looked at Ambrey. Her gaze remained locked on Arya as the bitch slowly crossed the platform.

"Like I said, I am not part of the girdack. Neither is Rogan." Ambrey's voice hadn't lost its growl.

Aeda, who'd remained close, turned toward her daughter.

"Fight her, Ambrey," Aeda said. "Face this challenge like you are meant to. You were born for this."

"I can't."

I glimpsed Ambrey's fisted hands and saw the fine tremors shaking her as she watched Arya. Ambrey was close to losing control again. I glanced at Arya and saw she had reached the edge of the platform. She blew me a kiss and jumped down with a bounce. Ambrey's tremors grew more pronounced.

"Of course you can," Ambrey's mother said sharply, reclaiming my attention. "You're choosing not to."

She started to reach for Ambrey, but I caught her wrist and pulled her hand back. Aeda looked at me in surprise.

"What do you think you're doing?" she asked.

"Protecting you."

She and the Lutha both scoffed. They had no idea.

Ayra, however, didn't share their mockery of my belief in Ambery. Arya's eyes narrowed on me, instead.

"Don't push Ambrey," I warned Aeda before letting go.

"I know my daughter better than you think. She may hate me, but she won't hurt me." She turned toward Ambrey. "We both know, this time, you can't say no."

Ambrey winced, brought a fist to her temple, and started to mumble.

"This is why I ran. Bitches in ditches. Dog fights and assholes. Nothing ever changes. Sucks you in but what will be spit out? Not what's wanted, that's what. Not happening. Not this time."

She let loose a frustrated roar that caused a few females in the crowd to shuffle further away. When Ambrey turned toward me, her eyes were anguished and pleading, confirming my suspicion that she didn't want to fight. I wished there was a way to stop it, but Aeda was right. Arya would never leave Ambrey's community alone if Ambrey didn't face her. And, Ambrey knew that just as well as I did.

"Rogan…"

I stepped toward her, but she held up her hand.

"Your word. Like last time."

The last time I'd given her my word, she'd been planning to confront Bull. She'd persuaded a few of his men to leave but had killed two of the humans in the room faster than I could think to move. She'd known it would be dangerous and hadn't wanted me to step in and risk getting hurt. What was she planning to do this time?

I glanced at Arya, who now stood several yards away, then back to Ambrey.

"You have my word."

TINK

Rogan's worry oddly soothed me. He cared about me, not the outcome of the fight. He and I were unlike anyone else in the girdack, and I loved him for that difference. To keep him and my community safe, I'd fight Arya. But, it would end there. I wanted nothing further to do with the girdack.

I met the Lutha's gaze. "Fine. I'll fight your daughter. But, remember what I said. I am not part of the girdack."

The Lutha gave a single nod that started everything in motion.

My mother pulled Rogan back a safer distance. Arya closed the distance between us.

"He won't smell like you for long," she said as we circled each other.

I said nothing, opening myself to her intentions. Her thoughts jumped around erratically. Most of it was blood and killing and eating. Then, they focused on me, on stepping forward and taking my neck between her hands. She couldn't decide if she wanted to squeeze the life out of me slowly or snap my neck for a quick ending so she could take Rogan immediately.

When her thoughts drifted to what she would do to Rogan, I lost it and punched her in the face. Her head snapped to the side and blood flew from her nose.

The murmur of conversation around me didn't break my focus as Arya's attention whipped back to me. She absently wiped the blood from her nose, and her thoughts concentrated on one action. She planned to hit me back.

As she swung, I ducked and planted my fist in her crotch. She cried out and started to fold in on herself. I straightened and hit her face again. More blood flew.

"Arya, focus," the Lutha barked.

Focusing wouldn't help her. Nothing but yielding would.

"Withdraw your challenge," I said, grabbing the taller woman's hair.

The sudden image of me on my back was the only warning I got before I flew over her shoulder. The impact knocked the wind from my lungs, but I didn't stay on the floor. Moving quickly, I flipped to my feet and went to kick Arya in the back. My skirt ripped and I felt a distinct breeze that had me changing from a kick to a punch. It wasn't nearly as effective, and the bitch whirled on me, fists raised.

"When he's in my bed, he will wear my marks for weeks. His chest. His back and ass. His legs."

Her words came with images. Rogan under her, begging her to stop as she marked him with her nails. Furrows of crimson. She would paint herself with the scent of his blood. She would break his legs to make sure he could never run from her again.

She moved closer, her taunting smile red with the blood from her dripping and swollen nose.

"Even with broken legs, he would try to run from you," I said.

In the moment of her surprise, I struck again. Instead of a fist, I swiped at her. Her quick reflexes saved her as she jerked back, and my claws only raked across her belly, tearing her shirt and ripping her skin. The furrows weren't deep.

She snarled and danced further backward before looking down at the bloody mess I'd made. The murmur of the crowd grew louder.

"Did she file her nails?"…"Are those really claws?"…"How is that possible?"

"Shut up!" Arya shrieked.

The crowd quieted, but it didn't matter. The questions had already distracted her. She wanted to break my fingers and rip my hands from my wrists.

"Bitch," she said, baring her teeth at me.

"Stop the fight now, Arya. Acknowledge Rogan is mine," I

said, giving her one last chance.

She flew at me, hands raised and fingers curled to rip apart my face. I shifted my weight to the side, evading her, and reached for her neck. With a powerful twist, I ended Rogan's ex.

A collective gasp rose. I released my hold on Arya and let her lifeless body fall. I felt no pride in the kill. It wasn't something my mother had ever understood. My ability to see what my opponent planned gave me an unfair advantage in every fight. Arya hadn't stood a chance. Just like my community wouldn't have stood a chance against her if I'd allowed her to live.

The people around us started talking all at once. Ignoring the noise, I looked at Rogan, hoping he'd understand I hadn't had a choice.

He gave me an encouraging smile, but I didn't smile back. This wasn't finished. Not yet.

I shifted my gaze to the Lutha. Her red mottled complexion as she stared at her dead daughter didn't bode well.

"Ambrey," my mother breathed, claiming my attention. Her smile was wide and her eyes glassy with unshed tears. "I knew you could do that. I always knew you were meant for so much more."

The Lutha twitched at her words.

"Mother. Shut up," I said softly.

Rogan grabbed my mom's arm and gently pulled her away from the Lutha, who was now completely focused on me.

"You had no right," she said, following the words with a low growl. "You are nothing, and she was next in line."

I remained quiet because no words would appease the woman. She wanted my head.

"End her," she snarled.

The five women on the platform, who'd done nothing since arriving, started toward me. I opened my senses further. Three had children at home. Their minds were on fighting smart and making it back whole and healthy to their young. Two thought only of how this fight would raise them higher in the Lutha's eyes. A familiar ache filled my head as I saw how they planned to attack. Hard and fast.

Five against one. Had I ever stood a chance coming here? Was my life one long tormented joke with only a few days of contentment?

I wouldn't live. The five had spoken ahead of time. One to go for the head, two to hold my arms, one to distract, and one to gut me.

Something cool brushed my mind, soothing my fear and agitation. The feeling spread, giving me strength and determination. With clarity, I saw what I needed to do.

"Megan will attack first," I said, watching the brunette. Megan pulled back her lip in a sneer but didn't slow. She jumped from the platform and flew at me. Her strength was an accurately placed strike to the temple, stunning her opponent.

I blocked her swing and swiped my claws across her throat. Her eyes widened and red blossomed as I spun toward the two who were already reaching for me, not yet aware that

Megan would not attack again.

"Two for my arms," I said, ducking under their reach and coming up with closed fists. The long bones in their upper arms snapped, the sound making me smile as Megan clasped her throat with a gurgle. One of the two women stepped back with a gasp, cradling her arm.

"I licked that bone on someone else once," I said. "I shouldn't have. I won't lick yours. Go home to your young."

The other two women who hadn't yet attacked, hesitated. But the second woman with a broken arm wasn't done. Her thoughts burrowed in my mind, and I turned toward her.

"I'll break the other one, too, if you'd like. Your mate won't appreciate changing diapers for that long."

She hesitated, and thoughts of another attempt faded from her mind.

"Pathetic," the Lutha said with a sneer at my attackers. "You do not deserve a position of power. You're weak."

The Lutha's thoughts touched me, and I turned to her.

"They aren't weak," I said. "You are."

A collective gasp rose from the crowd.

"Your plan won't work," I continued. "There are no others who will step forward to fight me. No one else to try to weaken me. You have two choices. Face me now or let us go for good."

Nine

TINK

"I will never allow you to walk away from what you've done," the Lutha said.

"What I've done?" I shook my head. "You sent Rogan running to me. You sent your daughter to stir up trouble to force me to answer your summons. You brought me here. You. Each injury and death is on your shoulders, not mine."

Her face turned redder with each word I spoke.

"What happens next will be on your shoulders, too. The choice is yours."

She barked out an angry laugh.

"You spout your shit as if anyone here cares what you say. This is my community. What I say matters here."

She stepped closer to me and looked at Megan, who lay lifelessly on the ground. The Lutha's thoughts, however, were not on the strongest of her members. Her thoughts remained eerily focused on Rogan.

"Why him?" I asked. "Why did he matter so much?"

The Lutha seemed to collect herself.

"He didn't matter. What mattered was his disobedience when he ran," she said, confirming my earlier thoughts.

Authority. That's all that mattered to her. That my accusations and then the death of her daughter had robbed her of even a piece of her authority was enough to push her to act directly.

And she couldn't stop thinking about her target.

ROGAN

The Lutha's gaze remained fixed on the dead woman separating her from Ambrey. The two with broken arms had quietly backed away while the two who'd never joined the fight had disappeared into the crowd.

Ambrey didn't look away from the Lutha or relax. Blood dotted Ambrey's face and blouse, the only signs she'd fought. The way Ambrey had met the attack, moving as she had, using her claws as she had...she was right; no one would challenge her. There was now no doubt in anyone's mind that she had the strength to take on the Lutha. And, the Lutha would never let that belief remain.

"Don't do it," Ambrey said softly, her gaze steady on the Lutha.

"Do what?" the Lutha asked, finally looking up from the body.

"Mother," Ambrey said. "Stand in front of Rogan."

Puzzled, I glanced at Aeda, who still stood beside me. She crossed her arms and shook her head.

"No. This is your challenge. Face it or lose him."

Him? Me? I looked at the Lutha as she laughed. One

moment she was near Ambrey, the next she was coming at me.

Hands gripped my arms and pulled me back as Ambrey growled and flew at the Lutha, intercepting the attack before the Lutha could touch me. My mother's scent and a pat on my arm as I was released was enough to assure me it was safe to keep my eyes on the fight.

The Lutha rounded on Ambrey with a strike to her face. Ambrey staggered a step, the only acknowledgment she gave the blow before snarling and lunging for the Lutha at the same time the Lutha swung toward Ambrey. The fight seemed choreographed.

The Lutha would attempt some form of attack, and Ambrey always knew just when to dodge. She'd often counterattack, but the Lutha seemed just as in tune with what Ambrey would attempt.

As they fought, something changed. My skin started to tingle. I broke out with goosebumps head-to-toe and sprang a painfully massive erection. I was still trying to figure out what the hell was wrong with me—who sprang wood in the middle of a challenge lethal enough to lose a mate?—when I caught sight of Ambrey's eyes. They glowed a soft amber.

My skin continued to tingle. I inhaled slowly and could smell her and the moon.

Just then, Ambrey crouched and spun, going under the Lutha's attack and raking her claws viciously across her middle.

The Lutha staggered back and clasped her stomach, red seeping from between her fingers.

"Bitch," she breathed. "They will kill you."

"No they won't. I'm not part of this. I never was, and I never will be."

The Lutha coughed and red painted her lips. Slowly her legs gave out, and she collapsed to the floor. No one moved forward to help her.

"He won't stay yours for long," she said, staring up at Ambrey. "You're not strong enough to keep him safe."

Ambrey frowned, and her hands started to shake.

"Everyone has ten seconds to clear the building," she said. "Anyone left inside will face me."

There was a shuffle of noise behind me. When I turned, over half the crowd had already cleared the doors.

"We'll be outside," my mother said before she and my father hurried to the door.

Aeda remained.

"Especially you, Mother," Ambrey said.

Aeda snorted. "You know I'm not interested in challenging you. You've done more than I'd ever dreamed possible, and you'll need my help maintaining control now."

Ambrey's head whipped toward Aeda, her still glowing amber gaze locking with the woman who'd birthed her.

"Maintain? No, Mother. I want no part of this."

"You can't be serious. You would walk away from your responsibilities as the new Lutha?"

My stomach twisted with the realization of what Aeda was saying. By killing the Lutha, Ambrey became the Lutha. Everything we'd both run from would be forced on us anyway.

"I made it very clear that I wasn't a part of the girdack.

The death of your leader is no concern of mine," Ambrey said, relieving me. "Now, leave. I want—"

Ambrey looked at me. The heat in her gaze made me want to drool and whimper at the same time.

"Ambrey, no. You need to control yourself and face—"

Ambrey growled a second before she moved. It was the only warning I had to get my arm up and block her hand from gripping her mother's throat. I grunted at the feel of her claws digging into my flesh but didn't pull away. Instead, I wrapped my other arm around Ambrey and turned her from her mother.

"Aeda, leave!" I shouted.

This time, the woman listened.

Ambrey snarled in my arms but didn't try to stop her mother. As soon as the door closed, I exhaled slowly and kissed the top of Ambrey's head. She continued to shake, each tremble tearing my skin further.

"Do you think you could let go now?" I asked softly.

She jerked her claws from my arm with a clipped apology but didn't move away from me. She stayed within my arms as if I had her trapped.

"Talk to me, Ambrey."

"I don't want to talk."

"Tell me what you need."

She looked up at me, her eyes still filled with power.

"You."

If I were a smarter wolf, I would have been worried. But I wasn't. Instead, I was hopelessly infatuated with this tiny woman with wicked claws that would likely leave a few additional scars before we exited the building.

"I need you, too," I said, lowering my lips to hers.

I kissed her hard and felt the sharp edge of her canines. She didn't kiss back or touch me. But when I pulled away, a warning growl rumbled in her throat.

"Is there a way we can do this so I can still walk out of the building on my own two legs?"

Ambrey winced slightly but nodded toward the back where a cement block wall rose floor to ceiling for the bathrooms.

"Good," I said.

She licked my chin then went to the wall, placing her open palms on the concrete. I followed closely and stared at the inch-long curved claws. Her power didn't intimidate me because she never wanted it to. Her caring and protectiveness had won me over long before we'd first mated. She didn't own me; we owned each other.

I tugged her skirt up around her waist, needing her right then as much as she needed me, and the sight of her pale round cheeks greeted me. I smoothed my hand over each, appreciating that they were already bare.

"Next time, I'm wearing underwear," she panted.

"No next time," I said, pulling back and easing down my zipper.

I never wanted to see her have to fight like that again. She'd hated it. I'd hated it, too.

"No next time," she agreed.

"And I hope you keep forgoing underwear because I really like being able to do this."

I clasped her hips, lifted her up, then pressed into her. The sound of her nails gouging the concrete motivated me to give her everything, to distract her from the fight and the power still coursing through her veins.

* * * *

I gave one last thrust and emptied myself with a groan. Neither of us moved as I twitched inside her. Slowly, my racing heart settled into a steady beat.

"Thank you, Rogan."

Honestly, I'd never been so grateful to hear something other than "again" come from her lips. She wiggled her hips loose and slid from my slick hold. When her feet touched the ground, she stood on the pants tangled around my ankles, preventing me from giving her some room. She didn't seem to mind. She turned and wrapped her arms around my waist.

"Are you ready to go home?" she asked.

"Soon," I said, kissing the top of her head. "I'm hoping we can stay at my parents' place for a few minutes so I can shower.

"Sounds good." She stiffened in my arms then pulled back to frown up at me. "I forgot about them."

I chuckled and smoothed back a few stray wisps of hair that had escaped her usually pristine bun.

"It's okay. They won't care about waiting. Not after what they witnessed here."

She let go of me and wiggled her skirt back down. When she stepped away, I wasn't as quick to yank my pants back up.

I gingerly eased my jeans over my hips and caught Ambrey's look of guilt before she glanced away.

"Don't let this fool you. I enjoyed every minute of that," I said.

She smiled briefly then focused on the bodies still in the center of the building.

"What do we do about those?" she asked.

I shrugged. "Like you said, not our business."

She nodded and waited for me to finish zipping.

Together we walked outside. The sun was much lower in the sky, but the air was still mellow with the heat of it. An older couple stood with my parents in the parking lot.

"Ambrey, these are the cleaners. If you're done inside, they will take over."

"We're done," Ambrey said.

My parents didn't move to walk toward the car as the other couple walked to the building. Mother waited until they were inside to address Ambrey.

"I'm sorry for challenging you yesterday. You are more than worthy of my son."

"Thank you," Ambrey said. "And thank you for protecting Rogan."

"Always," my mother said, starting toward the car. "Your mother left but asked that I give you a message."

"What's the message?" Ambrey asked as we followed.

"She'll be waiting for your call."

I snorted and got in the back with Ambrey. Given that I'd stopped Ambrey from killing her, Aeda would be waiting for that call for a long time.

"Are you hungry?" Dad asked from the front seat.

"Very," I said.

Ambrey remained quiet on the way home and through our quick late lunch. As soon as we were both showered and redressed, we said goodbye to my parents.

"There's no need for you to stay away now," my mother said, hugging me. "Come back when you can."

I glanced at Ambrey, unsure.

"We will," Ambrey said.

TINK

"What now?" Rogan asked as he backed out of the driveway.

"Now we go home."

I was eager to get back and check in on Shay, Will, and Denz. I hated leaving my community for any length of time. Trouble always seemed to pop up when I wasn't there. Well, it popped up when I was there, too.

"I know we're going home," Rogan said with a slight smile. "I also know we have enough food to last a few days when we get there." I didn't miss the husky tone in his voice. "But what then? We never talked about our future. What your mom said about you being the next Lutha got me thinking."

Worried, I studied Rogan's profile and opened myself to his thoughts. What I found stunned me.

He didn't have plans for me to become the next Lutha like

my mother did. His thoughts were focused on our community, where he already saw me as a Lutha of-sorts. He was wondering how long we would stay in the apartment, how many kids we would have, and what kind of job he would need to support his growing family.

I adored him.

"After making sure everything is all right, we're going to close our door for three days," I said.

"Three days? Not four?"

"Three," I said firmly. "I have responsibilities."

His thoughts narrowed to just kids and me walking around with a very large belly that he would touch and talk to constantly.

"How many children are you hoping we have?" I asked, curious. His mind wasn't specifically set on one number.

"Not sure. I guess it will depend on our means of supporting them." He glanced at me. "I've been meaning to ask...where did all that money come from?"

His thoughts turned to me working as a librarian stripper. I smiled.

"Thank you for not wanting me to change who I am."

"Never. I told you. You're perfect."

And in his eyes, I saw that I was.

"About that money?" he asked again.

"That's a story for another time."

Author's Note

Thank you for reading! If you liked Tink and Rogan, visit my website at http://mjhaag.melissahaag.com for updates on current projects and other books I've written.

Hope(less)
By Melissa Haag

Gabby's brain is like a human fish finder. It comes in handy when she wants to avoid people. Mostly men. They seem to like her a bit too much. It's lonely being different, but she's adapted to it. Really. She just wishes she knew why she is different, though.

In her search for answers, she discovers a hidden community of werewolves. She immerses herself in their culture, learning about their world until she meets Clay. He's unkempt, prone to mood swings, intense without saying a word, and he thinks Gabby is his.

It's going to take every trick she knows to convince Clay to go away, and every bit of willpower not to fall for him when she discovers the man beneath the rough exterior.

Delve into a riveting world of werewolves and young women with unexplained abilities, in Hope(less).

Printed in Great Britain
by Amazon